# On To
# Oregon!

John and Francis, long since, had learned how to load a
pack-animal, and though they now were obliged to work
by starlight, the job was done sufficiently well for the time
being. Catherine, with Matilda and Louisa, was mounted
on one ox; Francis, with Elizabeth, on the other. Then,
with the cow and oxen tied nose to tail, John, with the
baby in his arms, took the lead-rope and set off through the
sagebrush, heading due west.

It was a foolish, childish sort of plot. Everything was
against its success except that in a country so wild as this
all nature plotted with John to confuse and outwit the
grown people. A wind-storm rose with the sun and blew
the sand over the children's tracks....

# ON TO

# OREGON!

BY HONORÉ MORROW

ILLUSTRATED BY EDWARD SHENTON

A BEECH TREE PAPERBACK BOOK
NEW YORK

William Morrow & Company, Inc.
1350 Avenue of the Americas
New York, NY 10019.
Printed in the United States of America
First Beech Tree edition, 1991

10  9  8  7  6  5

To
Richard

# Contents

# Illustrations

# CHAPTER I

# The Beginning of the Trail

THIS is the story of a great boy pioneer. Perhaps there have been other boy pioneers, thirteen years of age, who were as great as John Sager, but, if so, I have not heard about them.

He was not a goody-goody sort of boy, you know. I suppose his manners, if he had any, were all bad. And, as you will see, his method of getting obedience from his brother and sisters was open to criticism. But he did a great job well; better,

I think, than any boy of today could hope to do
it. I think that was because John Sager lived under
conditions that made boys plan and do as boys are
not obliged to plan and do today.

He was born in Ohio, in 1831. His father, Henry
Sager, was a farmer and blacksmith. His mother,
Naomi Sager, was a fine housewife. When John
was seven, his brother Francis five, and his sister
Catherine four, the family migrated from Ohio to
a farm in Missouri.

John's earliest recollection of family talk was of
hearing his father trying to persuade his mother to
give up the Missouri farm and go with him to the
Oregon Country. John couldn't make out for many
years just what his parents meant by Oregon Country and he was inclined for a long time to agree
with his mother that it would be better to remain
in Missouri. Until a boy is about ten years old he is
very dependent on his mother, and her feelings and
opinions about family matters weigh more with
him than those of anyone else. So when John heard
conversations like this between his parents:

"But, Naomi, I talked today with a man who has
been clear through to the Pacific Coast. He says
that there's a valley that lies out near the coast,
on the other side of the Rockies, that's like heaven.
Flowers all the year round; soil black muck hundreds of feet deep; thousands of acres of it, to be

had for the taking. And, Naomi, *if we Americans
don't take it, the British will.*"

"But, Henry, the terrible journey between here
and that valley! Women and children couldn't un-
dertake it. You shouldn't ask it of me. After you
leave Missouri, you're at the mercy of the Indians
and the weather for two thousand miles. And that
article in the St. Louis newspaper said you can't
use a wagon after you reach the Rocky Mountains.
How would we get our furniture through? No! No!
Don't bother me with your restless talk."

When, I say, John first heard such exchange of
ideas as this between his parents, he was worried.
He shared all his mother's fears. Leave the Missouri
farm, the chickens, the calves, the dog, the flowers,
the bureau that held his clothes, and toys, the trun-
dle-bed in which he and his little brother Francis
slept so safely in the room with Father's and
Mother's big four-poster? John could not bear the
thought.

But his father had the born pioneer's firmness
of will. Not a week went by for years that he did
not talk to John's mother about Oregon, until the
idea of going there became a part of John's growing mind.

Their farm was located near the rough road that
led northwest toward the Platte River, and southeast to St. Louis. Over this road there traveled con-

stantly groups of trappers with pack-horses loaded
with furs which they had trapped in the distant
Rockies and were bringing to St. Louis. And over
the road, too, in the opposite direction, plodded
freighters' outfits, made up of covered wagons and
pack-mules carrying goods to Fort Laramie and
Fort Bridger, trading-posts far, far to the west, that
sought to exchange supplies with the trappers for
the precious furs.

Indians went up and down this road constantly.
All sorts and conditions of Indians. Sober chiefs
with their wives and children, their dogs, their
ponies following them in noisy confusion; young
braves, drunk and dangerous; Indian hunters carrying buffalo beef to St. Louis.

It was a fascinating road for a boy to watch. At
first John eyed it from the safe haven of his mother's
kitchen window. But as the years marched on, John
marched with them, away from his mother's skirts,
toward the split-rail fence that shut the farmyard
from the road, until, by the time he was twelve, he
sometimes went a mile or so along the road with
some outfit whose leader was willing to answer his
eager questions about Oregon. And then, before
she realized what was happening, John had crossed
over to his father's side of the Oregon idea, and
was teasing his mother to start for that fabled valley—the valley of the Willamette.

Now, in the five years that the Sagers had been living on this road, very, very few white women had traveled with the outfits that were heading for Oregon. A few missionaries' wives had gone through, but the average man hesitated to hamper himself with women and children on such a dangerous and difficult trip. And Naomi Sager clung to these facts when John and his father and even Francis nagged her to go West.

But even this argument was not to be left her. In 1843, Dr. Marcus Whitman, a missionary who with his wife carried on a thriving mission to the Indians near what is now Walla Walla, Washington, came through Missouri, urging families to follow him out to Oregon.

He told them about the wonderful climate, the vast rich lands, the mineral resources, and he told them over and over that unless hundreds of Americans got out there in the next year and took up land, the whole of Oregon Territory would go to the British. But, perhaps most important of all, Dr. Whitman said that wagons could go clear through to the Pacific Coast and that the trip was safe for women and children. In fact, he said he would lead a caravan through himself.

And that spring of 1843, there passed over the road by the Sagers' house the biggest outfit ever seen in those parts—a thousand men, women and children, with two hundred covered wagons, heading for Oregon under Dr. Whitman's leadership.

The talk of it and the sight of it set Henry Sager on fire. And, with all her pet arguments upset, poor Naomi Sager at last gave in. If, she said, a caravan as strong as the one of 1843 should be formed for 1844, she would join it.

Perhaps, poor soul, she thought no such great gathering of people could come together again. But she was wrong. In the spring of 1844, under the leadership of a man named Gillian, *fourteen hundred* people started for Oregon. And with them went the Sager family.

It was not the tiny family that had left Ohio six years before. The stork had called on the Missouri farm very regularly and had left Elizabeth, Louisa and Matilda. The huge covered wagon seemed to spout children at every opening. But there were many other big families in the caravan, and John was rather proud, in his secret heart, that none of them was larger than the Sagers'.

John, at thirteen, thought of himself as a man. As a matter of fact, he was still a little boy, in spite of his height of five and a half feet, because he still refused to take responsibility. He still expected his father and mother to act as his conscience. He still did as little as possible in the way of family jobs. Yes, the sure test of a boy's manliness is in his attitude toward his family, and by this test John was not as old as his sister Catherine, who at ten was a real little mother to the younger children.

All the way across the prairies of Missouri and Kansas, rich green against the May blue, John ran about the caravan carefree as a bird, leaving his chores to the younger children. His father, usually a strict disciplinarian, was, during those first few weeks of the journey, too much occupied with the heavy duties of the trail to keep an eye on John. But the day of reckoning came.

May weather had been beautiful and the caravan had made an average of fifteen miles a day. But June came in wet, and the bottom fell out of the prairie roads. The huge prairie schooners were as helpless in the mud as whales would have been. After three days of constant downpour, the caravan, instead of traveling in close formation, was strung out over ten miles of oozing road, with every driver of a wagon standing helpless beside a helpless team.

Henry Sager lashed and urged his great oxen until both he and the beasts were trembling with exhaustion. Mrs. Sager peered anxiously at him from beneath the wagon-hood. He was a big man, six feet tall, and every inch of those six feet was plastered with mud. His chestnut hair was full of it, and although he was clean-shaven his blue eyes

looked at her apparently over a close black beard.
His fringed buckskin coat oozed muddy water.

"Catherine!" called her father. "You go back and
drive herd for John while he comes up here to help
me. Francis still got stomach-ache, Mother?"

"Yes; he can't come out," replied Mrs. Sager.
Catherine, a blue-eyed, curly-haired child with
round red cheeks, thrust a leg in a red-striped
stocking out of the rear of the wagon, followed it
with the other leg, and slid to the ground. She was
wrapped in a piece of oilcloth.

The herds were kept in the rear of the outfit, but
the Sagers' was the end wagon. Catherine found
footing in the trampled grass by the roadside and
in five minutes had located John. He was playing
cards with several other herd boys under an abandoned wagon. When Catherine gave her message,
John rose slowly.

"You'll have to find the beasts," he said. "They're
back by that clump of cottonwoods yonder. Guess
you'd better drive 'em up nearer our wagon."

"You know I can't cut them out of the herd!"
cried Catherine. "You do it for me!"

"No, I got to go help Father." John spoke with
unusual alacrity, shaking the rain from his broad
felt hat, and pulling in his belt. He wore the usual
plainsman's outfit—a red flannel shirt with the tails
worn outside buckskin trousers, a wide leather belt

from which hung a knife, leather boots to the knee. He looked like Catherine except for the fact that his hair was not curly and that his red cheeks were spotted with freckles. "Don't you tell you found me playing cards," he added.

"I will if you don't help me get out our cows," declared Catherine.

John tossed his head and moved out of hearing of the other boys, who eyed him tauntingly Catherine, clutching the stiff brown oilcloth under her chin, followed him.

"I'm going back to the wagon with you!" she cried. "'Tisn't a mite of use my going into that hundred-head of cattle for ours, and you know it!"

"You'll do as I say or I'll slap your head off!" shouted John.

"Hateful, lazy thing!" shrieked Catherine, dancing out of his reach.

He did not follow her, for he exercised by virtue of brute force a crude sort of control over all the children but Francis. Francis was red-headed and unquenchable. John was sure that Catherine would not follow him.

Nor did she, immediately. She watched him set off for the wagon, then she began to run toward the cottonwoods, dim through the driving rain.

When John reached the wagon, his father was digging round the fore wheels with a shovel.

"Get the scythe out of the wagon and cut grass for me till I tell you to quit," he said. "Bring it in, armload at a time."

John jumped to obey with such swiftness that his father gave him a curious glance, but he made no comment. It was heavy work cutting the high, tough grass in the heavy rain. But John drove at it valiantly and shortly he bore back to the wagon a mighty armload. His father immediately began to pack it against the wheels. John was returning with his fourth load when Catherine appeared. She was panting so rapidly that for a moment she could not reply when her father said, sharply:

"What are you doing here?"

"I—can't—find—our—cows," finally gasped the little girl.

John's cheeks lost some of their fine glow. He dropped his load of grass and started hastily back toward his scythe; but his father spoke peremptorily.

"Hold up, John! Now, then, Catherine, what do you mean?"

"All the big herd's gone—all the hundred. I found the Penrose boy—tied up—in the cottonwood grass. He said Injuns came and tied him and drove off the herd. The other boys"—this with a taunting look at John—"were playing cards up under an old wagon."

Henry Sager seized John by the collar of his shirt.

"Give him a chance to say his say, Henry!" cried Mrs. Sager anxiously from the wagon.

"Chance!" snorted Henry Sager. He put two fingers of his free hand between his lips and blew a piercing blast. From the shadowy group about the next wagon emerged a figure on horseback. Another blast and another. The man galloped up. His beard was dripping wet, his gun ran a small rivulet over the pommel of his saddle.

"Indians have run the herd, Captain!" shouted John's father. "Don't know any details. Be with you in a minute!"

Captain Shaw, the head of the section of the caravan in which the Sagers traveled, left at a gallop. Henry Sager, with the assistance of a very rough knee, tossed John into the rear of the covered wagon.

"You stay there till I come back, without stirring or opening your mouth!" he cried. "Naomi, don't you go near him!"

His horse was staked by the roadside. He freed the tether-rope, vaulted into the saddle and was gone.

All the afternoon John sat on the washtub looking sulkily out over the misty plains. Francis, whimpering with stomach-ache, lay on a pile of blankets behind him, between the bureau and the big horsehair trunk. The little girls, with their mother's help

and that of Aunt Sally Shaw, the captain's wife, set
up the family tent beside the trail and began to
play school, while Aunt Sally and Mrs. Sager sat on
the front seat of the wagon and speculated on the
probabilities of the return of the herd.

Aunt Sally, ordinarily the most kindly of women,
said some very unkind things about the selfish heed-
lessness of boys. John scowled heavily. He had persuaded himself that he was very much abused.

"Don't expect a fellow to have any fun," his
thoughts ran. "Was guarding that herd from four
o'clock this morning. Funny if we couldn't take a
little rest. Wasn't my fault if Injuns took the old
cows. Good thing they're gone. Been nothing but
trouble and worry over 'em ever since we left home.
Have to keep 'em moving so fast don't give decent
milk anyhow. S'pose I'll get all the blame because I
was oldest of the herd gang. Good notion to run off
to an Injun camp and stay there."

He turned this over in his mind quite seriously
and managed to pass a considerable length of time
very pleasantly as he pictured himself as the white
chief of a conquering band of Red Men. His pleasant pictures were checked, however, when he heard
Aunt Sally say:

"I'm going to make some hot tea for all hands.
You're shivering, Naomi, and I declare I feel damp
in my very bones."

"That will be nice, Aunt Sally," replied John's mother. "We can eat some cold biscuit and dripping with it. . . . Don't bring any for John, though."

"Never fear!" exclaimed Aunt Sally.

John at once returned to his sulks. He was in a perfect fury of hunger, cold and resentment when his father returned. The rain had ceased with the coming of night. A cold wind blew from the west, where an orange glow gave promise of clearing weather. Mrs. Sager was cooking cornmeal mush over a miserable fire of wet cottonwood sticks, when Henry's weary horse halted in the smoke.

"Band of Indians holding the cattle for ransom in a little valley about ten miles north. I left Shaw and the rest to negotiate while I came back to tend to the oxen." Father Sager spoke in a voice of utter weariness.

"Here, have a bowl of mush. It'll put heart in you," said his wife.

"Have any trouble with John?" he asked grimly, as he devoured the great bowl of smoking food.

"Not a mite," replied Mrs. Sager. "I'm sure he's sorry."

"Humph!" grunted Henry Sager. He handed the empty bowl to Catherine, took the short quirt that hung from his saddle, and strode over to the wagon.

"Come down here, John," he commanded. "Now, sir," as John slowly obeyed, "you've been doing your best ever since we left home to earn a licking. You've thought that I was too busy to notice your deviltry, but mighty little has escaped me. You've been lazy and disobedient and you've been playing all kinds of smarty pranks with the other wagons. This business of the cattle caps the climax. Pull up your shirt and unfasten your breeches."

"Aren't you going to let me explain?" demanded John.

"It's too late for explanations," replied his father.

"At least, take me out of sight of the Shaw wagon!"

"Quit your nonsense!" shouted Henry, and lifted the quirt.

It was the most thorough drubbing John ever had received, and it was small consolation to know that somewhere along the trail his five companions in trouble were receiving the same sort of attention from their various fathers. When it was over, he was sent supperless to his bed of blankets under the wagon.

## CHAPTER II

# The North Platte

IT cost Henry Sager ten dollars to redeem his two cows. Ten dollars on the Oregon Trail in 1844 was a huge sum of money, and money was a scarce article in the Sager family. However, as was his custom, John's father made no reference to the matter. John had been punished, and the subject, so far as Henry Sager was concerned, was closed.

It was not closed with John, however. He nursed a bitter sense of resentment for days. His father had

forbidden him to leave the neighborhood of their
own wagon without permission during the remainder of the journey, and this helped to keep his sulking alive much longer than was normal with John.
He was by no means an ill-tempered boy, but he
had reached the age where childhood and dawning
manhood struggled against each other and he was,
for the time being, incapable of steady reasoning.
He made up his mind that since he was so utterly
misunderstood and unappreciated by his family he
would run away.

The muddy weather persisted for nearly the en-
tire month of June. John had no intention of starting
off in the rain. Trail life was too difficult under such
conditions. Moreover, as he listened to the conver-
sation of the men who dropped back to get his
father to do blacksmithing jobs for them during
the noon halt or after the night camp had been set,
he concluded that this country of the Platte River,
with its vast alkaline wastes, was no place for a
boy to sustain life with the meager outfit he was
gathering together and hiding in the box his father
allowed him to keep under the bureau.

The loneliness of the country through which they
were traveling was frightful. Fort Leavenworth, on
the eastern border of Kansas, was the last sign of
civilization the caravan had seen, and no other
would appear until they reached Fort Laramie, a

fur-trading station kept by a Frenchman in what is
now eastern Wyoming. If John had been able to lay
hands on plenty of powder and shot, he would have
been far less fearsome, for there were prairie-dogs
everywhere about—and they were reaching buffalo
country. But Henry Sager cherished his tiny supply
of ammunition as carefully as he did the pieces of
gold which he wore in a belt next his skin. So,
taking one consideration with another, John decided
to put off his disappearance until they reached Fort
Laramie, where there were trappers and friendly
Indians in the mountains.

The caravan should have reached Fort Laramie
by the first of July, or even earlier. This was necessary if it was to pass through the Snake River country and over the Blue Mountains before the October
snows were due. But the rains of June delayed it,
and by July it had only reached the forks of the
Platte, a good week's journey from the fort.

John's sullenness worried his mother. It was
something new with the boy in his relationship to
her. She asked him several times what was troubling
him, but received only a half-impertinent, half-surly
reply. Then she tried coddling him a little; would
secretly give him a bit of sweet dough or an extra
buffalo-rib which she had saved from her own share
of the meager family menu. Boylike, he accepted
these, but returned at once to his pose of injured

dignity. In an ugly way, John was having a good time.

He and Francis and young Elizabeth, aged seven, had a sort of unwritten, unacknowledged rule. Their mother was gentle and patient, so they never obeyed one of her orders unless she repeated it at least twice. This rule, of course, did not hold when their father was within hearing. For he was, in spite of his genial wit and affectionate nature, a stern man, with no patience whatever with the children's naughtiness, particularly toward their mother.

John's sullenness did not worry his father. He had a clear recollection of his own boyhood. He did not try to make friends with the boy, knowing that any such attempts would only add to John's belief in his own righteousness and importance. He allowed him to keep to himself all he wished, only insisting that he appear promptly at meals and at morning prayers.

No matter how hurried the morning departure, or how bad the weather, Henry Sager, each day before breakfast was eaten, read a chapter from the Bible and obliged the children to say the Lord's Prayer in unison. There was many another family in the caravan which began the day in this manner. It is an interesting fact to remember that, from the Pilgrim Fathers down through the centuries, many of the most difficult settlements of America have been made by people who believed in worshiping God daily.

John, who during the thirteen years of his life could not recall a single morning when he had not listened to his father's Bible reading, discovered suddenly that he was ashamed of family worship. Some of his new friends had laughed at him for attending anything so "soft." Not only was he ashamed of it, but he was dreadfully bored by it. He believed that he must have heard the Bible read through half a dozen times.

One morning, about a week before the caravan reached Fort Laramie, John deliberately dawdled over his currying of the oxen after his father had opened the Bible. Henry Sager, red flannel shirt a deeper red in the rising sun, his clean-shaven face full of tired and anxious lines, stood beside the fire, the big Bible in both hands. Mrs. Sager sat with the other children about the great square of oilcloth spread on the grass, which did duty as both table and spread.

"Hurry, John!" called his father.

John lifted his good-looking, sulky face over Hiram's broad brown back. "I'm too busy to listen to that old Bible this morning," he grumbled.

Curious that a man so large as Henry Sager could be so quick on his feet that often a boy as agile as John could not dodge him. With two leaps that car-

ried him over the fire and around the ox, he had
John by the ear. A moment later, John, holding his
ear, was sitting in his place at the table listening
for the seventh time to the story of the ten lepers.

It was a bad beginning for the day and helped
John to make the wild decision he made that evening. Unfairly enough, the trouble in the evening
was caused by his mother. Just as the camp was set,
a herd of buffalo appeared on the horizon to the
east. Henry Sager left the two boys behind to do
his share of the evening chores and joined Captain
Shaw in the wild gallop after the herd.

Their father was not out of sight when young
Francis and John began to argue. Francis, small
for his age, with big gray eyes that seemed to
take up more than their share of his little freckled
face, appealed after a moment to his mother.

"Hasn't John got to help gather buffalo chips? He
says if he stakes out the oxen, that's enough. But I
have to milk the cows, so I have just as much extra
work as John. We both ought to gather buffalo chips
like we always do."

"Oh, don't argue, boys!" sighed their mother.
"The girls and I will gather the chips."

She lifted the bushel basket as she spoke and,
followed by the flock of little girls, began to gather
the dry buffalo dung, which was the only available
fuel. Three baskets was the amount required to

cook a meal. John and Francis, quite content with
the arrangement, turned to attend to their father's
chores. John finished staking the oxen and was
standing by the fire watching his mother bring in
the third basket of chips, when she called to him.

"John, please go down to the river for a pail of
water."

John did not budge.

"Run along, dear." His mother was panting with
the load of chips.

"Aw, let Francis go!" drawled John.

At that moment, something struck John on the
ear. He thought for a second that a horse had run
into him. But as he sought to rise, he discovered
his mistake. His father had returned through the
dusk for his hunting-knife—the kill had been made
quickly. As John rose, his father took him by the
arm. "So, sir, you *will* stand by the fire and watch
your mother heave that basket for you? You *will* let
her plead with you for a bucket of water, you—"

Mrs. Sager rushed forward. "Please, Henry!
Please! I just can't bear another scene!"

Henry Sager looked down at her sweet face, his
own twitching with anger. "Very well," he said
abruptly. "Get out of my sight, you lazy hound,
then." And he strode off to finish his butchering.

When he was out of hearing, John shook his fist

"I won't stand it!" he cried. "I won't stand any more of his bullying!"

"He doesn't give you half you deserve!" shrilled Catherine, then darted out of reach of his hand.

John turned on his heel and climbed into the wagon. He took from his box the little bag of bullets he had collected, and the powder-horn. He hung these to his belt. Into his pocket he put a flint and steel, over his shoulder, a water-bottle and a blanket-roll, and took his gun on his back. Then he sneaked out of the front end of the wagon and started for Fort Laramie.

It was necessary, of course, for him to make a wide circuit of the camp, which was not easy. A camp of fourteen hundred people, with the cattle and outposts belonging to it, is not easy to leave or pass unobserved. But John managed it.

With the enormous aptitude of boyhood for such matters, he had by this time become an excellent trail man. Clear of the camp, he put the north star over his right shoulder and struck into the sagebrush wastes. He was not afraid of immediate pursuit. His family would think he had merely disobeyed again and had returned to some of his forbidden friends. So, after walking steadily for a couple of hours, he spread his blanket under a six-foot clump of sagebrush and, in spite of his excitement and fear of Indians, he went to sleep.

He was awakened at dawn by a hand over his mouth. An Indian, with a long scar on his cheek and a toothless grin, was bending over him. John lay motionless with fright. The Indian raised his hand and slapped John several times on the mouth, at the same time shaking his head. John knew that he was being ordered to keep silent and he tried to show his understanding by nodding. The Indian grunted and began to peel John's clothes from his trembling body. When the boy was stark naked, his evil-smelling visitor, who himself wore a ragged suit of beaded buckskin, rolled the clothing and blanket round the water-bottle and the belt with the knife and ammunition, tucked the bundle under his arm, picked up the gun, and suddenly vaulted to the back of a half-starved pony drooping beside the sagebrush clump.

Anger suddenly overcame John's terror. He bounded to his feet with a roar. But the Indian, with a cackle of laughter, was gone. John took a single leap after the flying horse—and stopped. The ground all about him, where it was not overgrown with sagebrush, was dotted with prickly cactus, and his single leap had filled his right foot with thorns. He supported himself against a sagebrush with one hand, nursing the foot with the other, while he looked about him.

He was standing on the top of a wide slope,

whitened with alkali and the bleached bones of
thousands of buffalo. Looking down the slope, to
the north lay a crooked silver ribbon, the Platte,
making its tortured way between flat banks. Beyond
the river lay vast slopes like that on which John
stood, losing themselves at last in dim red hills.
But all that interested John in the desolate land-
scape was a slow-moving line of black-and-white
dots along the south bank of the river. It was the
caravan, starting on its day's journey.

The sun was an hour high and the caravan was
all in motion. No, not all. There was a wide gap
between the end of the moving line and the last
wagon, a gap from which rose the dust of the cattle-
herd. And that last wagon did not move.

Some instinct told John that that wagon was the
Sagers', told him so although it might as well have
been any other of the two hundred-odd wagons in
the caravan. He wondered if they were waiting
for him, or if someone, his mother, were ill. Suddenly John was the most ashamed boy in all the
United States, including the Louisiana Purchase.
But he was really ashamed of being naked and of
having been robbed by an Indian. He wasn't in the
least remorseful for having run away, nor was he
in the least degree persuaded that his father had
been justified in punishing him. But he realized that
he was in a serious situation and that his one hope

was to reach that wagon, which, as the great caravan moved on, was more and more solitary.

The July sun beat so strongly on his back that
he crouched in the shadow of the bushes. Tiny black
flies by hundreds began to nibble at his sensitive
skin. Lizards scuttled across his defenseless feet.
He was hungry and thirsty. John was not happy.

His first shamed thought was that he would hide
until sundown, then sneak back over the six or seven
miles which lay between him and the wagon and
somehow lay hold of some clothing before he was
discovered. But his second thought made him realize
that in his unprotected condition, the thorns with
which this terrible country protected itself would
tear his skin to shreds and utterly cripple his feet;
that travel by daylight was his only chance to travel
at all. Even at that, he must move, sun and thirst
tortured. He started down the slope, watching every
step, but every step was torment, and his progress
was at a snail's pace.

It must have been about ten o'clock in the morning that John crouched under a bush for a short
rest. He was in a deep fold or crack in the slope
which ran parallel to the river for many miles. If
he had been going to Fort Laramie, thought John,
this would have made a wonderful hidden trail. He
felt quite secure from Indians here, and closed his
burning eyes—only to open them at once, for he

heard the soft thud of a horse's hoofs coming from
the southeast. He peered stealthily from his shelter.
A white man, his gun across his knees, was ap-
proaching at an easy trot. John bounded to his feet
and waved a frantic and grimy paw.

"Hey, Mister! Mister!"

The man's pony shied. The man's finger came
to rest on the lock of his gun, then shifted as he
grinned at the strange figure shrinking among the
greasewood thorns. He was a keen-looking man of
less than thirty, with fine blue eyes beneath level
brows, and a thin, clean-shaven jaw. He wore
fringed buckskins. A string of Indian scalps hung
from the pommel of his saddle.

"Blistered if it isn't nothing but a boy!" exclaimed
the stranger. "How come, boy?"

"An Indian robbed me this morning," cried John.

The stranger looked around him. "Where's your
camp? Who're you with?"

"I'm alone," replied John, with what dignity he
could gather together.

"So I see. But how come you to be alone? Belong
to that big outfit up ahead, I suppose. Got lost, did
you?" The keen eyes searched the boy's.

John blushed, hesitated, and suddenly decided
to make a clean breast of it. The man would learn
the facts later, anyhow.

"I had a lot of trouble with my folks and decided

to strike out for myself. I was on my way to Fort Laramie to get a job as a trapper."

"Uh-huh!" grunted the stranger. "Told your folks you were going to make a sneak of it?"

"I—I didn't tell them," mumbled John.

"How old are you, young fellow?"

"I'm thirteen."

"Oh! I see. You look older. Hum! Well, what do you expect me to do?"

"Give me a drink of water, please, Mister!" exclaimed John; "and if you could let me have a piece of blanket to cover me, I'd see that you got paid as soon as I get a job."

"If I do that, what'll you do next?" asked the stranger, still watching the boy's freckled, dirty face.

"Well, I'll get back to my folks. I think that's their outfit way down yonder."

"Down yonder! What do you mean?" asked the man.

"I mean that lone wagon by the river," replied John. "Haven't you seen it?"

"I've been traveling this draw since dawn," exclaimed the stranger, suddenly urging his horse to the edge above. He gave a quick look at the wagon, and then turned to John, who had followed him.

"If I help you out, will you go back to the wagon and not run away again?"

"I'm not going to stay at home if my father keeps on bullying me. I'm too old to be licked!" John's blue eyes blazed angrily.

"Then you'll get no help from me," said the stranger, touching his horse with his spurs.

"O Mister, wait!" wailed John.

The man pulled in his horse and with a look half contemptuous, half amused, turned in his saddle. "You are big enough in size not to get any more lickings, but I'll bet your mind is about ten years old! If 1 were your daddy, I'd lick whey out of you night and morning. Think of a boy who's been on the trail three months or so not having learned enough to know his only chance to live was to stick to the outfit! You puling brat! Well, what do you want?"

"I'll promise not to run away till we reach the Willamette Valley if you'll help me out," John said between his teeth, hating all grown men in the world.

"That's good enough!" The stranger smiled pleasantly. "As you see, I'm traveling light, but I'll do what I can for you." He swung easily off his horse as he spoke. "My name's Kit Carson. What's yours?" He handed John his water-bottle.

"John Sager," replied the boy, looking at him in awe. He had heard of this man as he had heard of all the other famous scouts of the Rockies. The men and boys in the caravan talked much of them. John knew that Carson was said to be the finest horseman in the West and that the Indians were supposed to fear him more than they feared any other American.

Carson undid his saddle-roll. It contained a red flannel shirt and a pair of moccasins. "This is all I have extra. Put them on. Put your hand in that bag. It's full of jerked beef."

John obeyed both orders with lightning speed.

"Now, this isn't a healthy spot to tarry in. A band of Sioux has been following the big caravan for two days. I guess the caravan can look out for itself better than that little outfit below, though. What a passell of fools!" The scout replaced the blanket-roll. "Hop up behind me, John. We've no time to waste."

It was noon when Carson and John jogged into Henry Sager's camp. Henry came out of the tent. He did not speak to John, but held out a great hand to Carson.

"Howdy, sir! Much obliged to you. I'm Henry Sager. 'Light and eat."

"My name's Carson. Mr. Sager, there's a band of Indians about five miles on the back-trail. You'd better hitch and drive like the devil till you overtake the big outfit. You shouldn't have got separated from it."

Under his tan, Henry Sager's face went white. "I know, but we had—well, a baby arrived this

morning and about an hour later my oldest daughter
broke her leg climbing out of a moving wagon.
Keep out of there, John!" he added, as John edged
toward the tent.

Kit Carson's voice was suddenly full of sympathy.
"That's hard. No doctor, I suppose."

"Yes, it happened before the caravan moved. Big
Dutch doctor—said he was a doctor anyhow—took
care of my wife and set Catherine's leg. Mrs. Shaw's
with us—wife of our company captain. Guess we got
to be moving, whether or no. John, Francis, bring
up the oxen! Wife's in the wagon. Daughter's in
the tent."

Kit Carson stood for a moment in thought. "Someone ought to warn the main outfit, but I guess that's
too late. Call in the boys. Get your gun. Arm the
boys and Mrs. Shaw, if they can shoot."

Henry Sager followed Carson's quick glance toward the river. Up its banks rode six Indians in
feathered war-bonnets. Sager ran to obey Carson's
orders. Carson himself, with a sudden unearthly
yell, galloped toward the Sioux. At sight of him
they drew up their horses. He stood in his stirrups
and shot, first his gun, then his two pistols. Two
Indians rolled beneath their ponies' hoofs. The
others turned and fled. Carson rode briskly up to
the fallen braves.

Ten minutes later he rode into the Sager camp,

leading two ponies, three guns across his knees, and two new scalps dripping blood from his pommel.

John, still in Carson's shirt and moccasins, had been placed by his father at the rear opening of the wagon, with Francis' gun in his hands. Within the wagon were packed the two women and the other children. Henry Sager guarded the front opening.

"Well," said Carson, "you'd better finish hitching up and get going. They won't bother us for a while, anyhow."

The two boys rushed out to the oxen. Henry and Carson struck the tent and tossed the pots, dishes and clothing which littered the camp, into the wagon.

As they sought vainly to hurry the oxen into their yokes, Francis for the first time spoke to John.

"Baby boy lost his panties, eh?"

"You'd better keep off'n me!" returned John. "This shirt belongs to Kit Carson! So do the moccasins!"

"Gosh!" breathed Francis, his gray eyes wide with sudden envy. "Did you swap with him? Wouldn't he put in the breeches, too?"

"Boys!" shouted their father. "Get those beasts going!"

John, his red shirt-tails flapping about his bare knees, thrust the wagon-tongue into place and

Francis cracked the black whip. The wagon lunged forward through the dust. Henry Sager, his gun over his shoulder, took his place to the right of the team.

"John," he said gruffly, "your mother wants to see you. Get into your own clothes and return those to Mr. Carson. Then get back and drive herd with him. I'll tend to your case later."

John, face purple, clambered into the moving wagon through the rear opening.

It was not as disorderly within as one might imagine. The three little girls, Elizabeth, Louisa and Matilda, with Mrs. Shaw, were packed together on the front seat. In the space between the bureau, trunks and chairs lashed to either side of the wagon, on deep-piled blankets and quilts, John's mother and Catherine lay foot to foot, Mrs. Sager with her head toward the front seat, Catherine's tousled brown braids rubbing the tail-board.

John made his way carefully, as the wagon swayed and bounced, between Catherine and the horsehair trunk, and crouched on the blankets beside his mother. She had lovely hair, curly and light chestnut in color. It lay in a great braid over her shoulder and curled in soft little ringlets about her delicate face. Her eyes just matched the deep blue of the sky that shone through the wagon opening. Her mouth was beautifully curved and very sweet in expression.

As John dropped down beside her she laid a weak hand on his brown paw.

"What happened to you, my son?" she asked.

John flushed uncomfortably. "I told you I wasn't going to stay to have him lick me all the time," he mumbled.

"John, he loves you dearly. He was almost frantic when he found you'd run away."

"Yes, he must've been! Says he'll tend to my case later. Nice, cheerful thing for me to look forward to!"

"Can't you understand, dear?" pleaded his mother. "He has such terrible responsibilities and you won't do a thing to help that we don't drive you to."

John's lips set sullenly. The demon that belongs to the boy of thirteen still held him in its black spell. He saw nothing but himself and his own desires.

His mother's eyes filled with tears. "I haven't the strength to argue with you or to hear what happened to you. But promise that you'll not run away again."

"I already bargained with Kit Carson not to go till we reach the Willamette," replied John.

His mother smiled and patted his hand. "Don't you want to see your new little sister, dear?"

"Gosh, another girl!" groaned John.

This time his mother actually laughed as she
turned back the covers and showed him the little
face nestled on her arm. "Poor John! Never mind!
Some day you'll feel differently."

His mother's laughter was hard to resist. John
grinned sheepishly, glanced quickly about to make
sure that he was not observed, and gave his mother
a hasty kiss.

"I gotta git my good pants," he said, scrambling
to his feet. "An Indian stripped me. These clothes
are Kit Carson's."

His mother's eyes for a moment reflected the terror she felt at what he had escaped. But the next
moment she was smiling again. "Lower bureau
drawer," she said.

John sat down beside Catherine to pull on his
breeches. Her eyes and cheeks were bright with
pain.

"Hurt much?" asked John.

"It's just awful! Worse with this old wagon hit-
ting me around."

John stared at her thoughtfully; then he pulled
his box from beneath the bureau and rummaging in
its depths he pulled out what looked like a little roll
of newspaper. He tore the paper carefully away
from the treasure it enfolded and disclosed a stick
of hoarhound candy.

"Here," he said gruffly. "I was saving that to trade

with the Injuns when we got to Fort Laramie. You can make it last for hours if you suck it slow."

"Do I have to give it back?" cried Catherine exultantly.

"No, it's yours," replied John, tossing his head as if candy were nothing to him.

"I'll do a lot of chores for you when I get well," said the little girl, taking an ecstatic lick at the hoarhound.

"Shucks!" John began to whistle and dropped out of the wagon.

His father at once ordered him to take Francis' place driving the oxen, for though he could make as much noise as any grown man, Francis was too small to wield the whip effectively.

# CHAPTER III

# Fort Laramie

ALL the burning afternoon and until ten o'clock that night, without stop save to ease the panting team, they hurried through the choking alkaline dust. At ten they came upon the first outpost of the caravan camp and a little later

took their place within the circle of wagons that
belonged to Captain Shaw's company, and Carson
went to seek General Gillian.

John, too weary to heed the preparations for attack that shortly roused the great camp, crawled
under the wagon, rolled himself in his blanket and
went to sleep. He was roused at dawn by the crackle
of gun-fire. As his father had bade him the night
before, he immediately crawled into the wagon and
took his station at the tail-board, with his gun. Here
he shivered and shuddered for a long quarter of
an hour, watching the red light of dawn pick out
wagon after wagon, and wondering how it would
actually feel to shoot a man.

But, happily, he was given no opportunity. Kit
Carson, at midnight, had stolen from the camp with
fifty mounted men, heading them out into the silent
plains to the west and concealing them in the sagebrush. The Sioux, stealing up from the south, had
scarcely begun their attack, when Carson's band
swept around behind them and, echoing the scout's
terrible war-cry, opened fire.

Of all that band of two hundred braves, not a
dozen escaped. The caravan lost two men and had
a dozen wounded for Dr. Dutch, as the big German
doctor was called, to exercise his none too great skill
upon.

Mrs. Shaw had returned to her own wagon the

night before, but as soon as the attack had ended, she appeared in sunbonnet and clean blue calico apron. She was ruddy-faced and blue-eyed and cheerful. She bade the boys get the breakfast fire started, and hunger drove them to instant obedience. They even got the kettle to boiling, and Francis was attempting to fry cornmeal mush when, having attended to the invalids, Mrs. Shaw came out to lend a hand.

When Captain Shaw, with Kit Carson and Henry Sager, appeared, the breakfast was waiting for them. To John's great embarrassment, his father opened the big Bible. And to his still greater astonishment Kit Carson asked his father to read the prayer of Habakkuk. "My favorite verses in the Bible," he said in his gentle drawl. A scout who knew and liked the Bible! John felt utterly confused.

At the end of the meal the Shaws rushed off to start their wagon and the scout announced his intention of hurrying on to Fort Laramie.

"I'm looking for a man," he said in his soft slow voice. "I've got to quit fooling and move along or I'll miss him."

"Someone you got to kill?" inquired Francis eagerly.

"No, young fellow. I don't kill white men," replied Carson with a smile.

"I'm not going to try to thank you, sir," said

Henry Sager, "for all that you've done for me and mine. Some day I'll hope for a chance to do you a big turn."

"Don't thank me. Thank John!" returned the scout. "If he hadn't held me up out there in the bushes, I'd have gone straight on to the main caravan."

"Is that so?" exclaimed Henry Sager.

"It sure is! Better not give him that lickin' I see in the back of your eye, sir." Carson's keen eyes were very kindly.

John held his breath and tried to look innocent and injured at the same time. Suddenly his father laughed.

"Well! Well! Guess I'll have to give in this time! Get the oxen up, Johnny!"

And so the bad moment passed.

The remainder of the journey to Fort Laramie was without event. Under their father's stern and watchful eye, John and Francis did poor little Catherine's hateful chores, dishwashing and helping with the cooking. The cooking their father did himself, and he was not a half bad cook, it was discovered. The baby was a week old and Mrs. Sager was sitting on the front seat, packed in pillows, by the time the famous trading-fort was reached.

After the weeks and months during which no human habitation had been seen, this fort, set on

the bank of the Laramie River, surrounded by the
Black Hills and with the beautiful Laramie Peak
as a background, seemed to John a very wonderful
place. Yet it was made only of adobe: thick walls
about twice the height of a man, built in a square
about half the size of a small city block. Within
were several tiny one-room houses where the chief
trader and his clerks lived. There were many lodges
of friendly Indians without the fort, and while the
caravan was coming into camp near by, these Indians swarmed over the wagons, looking for a
chance to trade pelts for food.

But food supplies in the caravan were running
low. The long delays caused by the rains had eaten
into the reserves of every family. The immigrants
had nothing to swap with the Indians. Their eyes
were fixed on the trader in the fort. But, to their
consternation, they found the prices were beyond
most of them. Flour was forty dollars a barrel. Sugar
was a dollar and a half a pound.

Henry Sager, with his wagon full of little hungry
mouths, was angry and attempted to argue with
the chief trader. But that gentleman could not be
moved.

"I bring this stuff over the same route you came,
stranger," he said. "I can sell every ounce of it at
this price. I ain't in this business for charity."

Very grimly, John's father counted out four ten-dollar gold-pieces and hoisted a barrel of flour to his shoulder, while John trotted beside him carrying his father's gun as well as his own.

"We'll live on buffalo meat, John, you and I and Francis, and leave the flour to Mother and the girls," said Henry Sager.

John nodded. Nothing mattered to him for the moment except the fact he had just learned. Kit Carson had left Fort Laramie and gone on to Fort Hall, over a month's journey to the west. The blue-eyed scout, with his gentle manners, had become a sort of god to John. He was delighted when he heard Captain Shaw order the company to be ready to move the next morning, and laughed when he heard the general grumbling. Everyone had hoped for at least three days' rest.

The high prices of food at the fort meant that most of the people were beginning to be hungry and that more and more time had to be given to hunting buffalo. Hunger and the loss of time, for the cold nights already gave a hint of trouble ahead, worked havoc with people's nerves. There was a good deal of quarreling between the wagons; and Captain Shaw, an old soldier who had fought under General Jackson in the War of 1812, had to establish military discipline in his company to keep it in order and steadily moving.

The country west of Fort Laramie was known as

the Great American Desert. The trail led, for the
most part, along the North Platte, over ground so
rough and alkaline that the livestock all began to
suffer from sore feet. Worse than this, dysentery
made its appearance in the caravan, and Dr. Dutch
rode up and down the line all day long, with a jug
of castor-oil hanging on one side of his saddle and
one of peppermint-water on the other.

For some reason, the Sager girls did not contract
the disease. But John and Francis lay ill in the
wagon for a week after leaving Fort Laramie, and
they were barely able to return to their share of the
family chores when their father crept into bed beside Catherine and lay there in agony while Dr.
Dutch dosed him.

The big German greatly liked and admired Henry
Sager, and had a real affection for the gentle Mrs.
Sager. But he did not attempt to conceal the fact
that he considered John an ill-trained cub. No German boy, he told the children, ever would have such
impolite manners to his father and mother.

His disapproval of John, however, did not prevent
Dr. Dutch from being wonderfully kind to the family. After he had made Henry Sager as comfortable
as possible, he insisted on driving the team, for the
boys were still too weak for that long day's tramp
over the difficult trail. But the doctor was no driver
of oxen and this was no part of the trail to entrust

one's wagon and life to a green hand. The caravan had now left the Platte River trail and was actually entering the gigantic rise of the Rocky Mountains. It was a country of marvelous beauty, with huge, snow-capped peaks lifting their heads one after another from the sky-line, as they pushed ever westward and westward. Awful canyons obstructed the trail. Strange rock forms of every color rose to right and left—towers and turrets in wild twisted shapes of orange and red and black.

The famous Oregon Trail was really no trail at all in 1844; that is, after Fort Laramie was passed. Along sandy levels the caravan could follow the ruts made by Dr. Whitman's migration the year before. But when the way led over mountains of broken rock, across boiling rivers, gashed out of solid stone, or along some hideous precipice, there was no trace left of the previous passing and each wagon shifted for itself.

And it was over such country that Dr. Dutch undertook to drive the Sagers' wagon. At first, the oxen wouldn't move at all for him, for he couldn't manage the black whip and they didn't understand the German for "Gee!" or "Haw!" But he finally solved this problem by carrying great pocketfuls of stones with which he pounded their sensitive flanks, and they would actually leap and plunge like colts. And this was not the sort of driving one enjoyed,

when the outer wheels of the wagon were within an inch of a canyon-edge half a mile deep. After a few hours of it, John was begging the doctor to return to the patients who were clamoring for him in other sections of the caravan. But Dr. Dutch was enjoying himself. He had neither family nor wagon of his own. A big bay horse which he loved as if it were a human being, and his saddle-bags and blanket-roll, represented all that he was taking into the Oregon country. He had the fine, sturdy love of pioneering that belongs to the Teutonic race wherever it finds itself, and he laughed at John and ordered him back into the wagon.

Now, John was in that curious state of mind in which a boy violently resents not being treated like a man. He had come to the conclusion that the only person in the world who understood and appreciated him was Kit Carson, and he was comparing every man he knew with the scout. Of course, no man measured up to Carson. His father? Certainly not, thought John. His father was bigger and perhaps better-looking than Kit, but his father was harsh and made his children work too hard. Captain Shaw, General Gillian, were good men in their ways, but in breaking up the Indian attack as he had, the scout had made these old soldiers appear like babies. Carson had made his father admit that he, John Sager, had saved the whole Sager family from the Indians. And now, here was this German doctor treating him like a baby, while his stupid driving risked the lives of the Sagers again. Well, John would show this doctor! Once more he would save the family, ungrateful though it always had been to him.

He was sitting on the front seat of the wagon as these thoughts traveled through his mind. His mother was sitting beside his father and Catherine. Francis was asleep. He crawled down from the wagon and dropped back to the rear where Dr. Dutch's horse was tied by a long rope to the tailboard. Everywhere along the way grew cactus of varied and menacing form. With his knife, John cut a burr with thorns the size and strength of small carpet-tacks. Bearing this on the point of his knife, he crept up to the doctor's horse and slipped the burr under the saddle. The horse reared. And as he reared, John cut the halter-rope. Instantly, plunging and snorting with pain, the horse galloped wildly off at right angles to the trail.

John crept back to his place on the front seat, then shouted, "Doctor! Doctor! Isn't that your horse running away?"

"Gott in Himmel!" roared the good doctor, as he followed John's pointing finger. "Shtop him! Here, vait a minute! Vait a minute! Someone loan me a horse!"

"Take my father's!" cried John. "I'll take care of the oxen for you."

A moment later Dr. Dutch was hurtling among the tumbled heaps of rocks that already concealed his beloved horse. John picked up the black whip, quieted the uneasy oxen, and began to follow the cavalcade up the wild reaches of the South Pass, the crest of the Rocky Mountains.

As children's plans are apt to be, John's was clever for the moment, but it was not far-sighted. It served to keep the doctor away from the wagon all day while John, with real skill, guided the oxen to the top of South Pass. But the doctor had been right when he had insisted that John was not well enough to plod beside the ox-team all day, and by night he was in a raging fever and the dysentery had returned to him full force. He was barely able to wheel the wagon into its place in the circle, before he fell to the ground, too ill to move. His mother, with Francis' feeble help, rolled him into a blanket and gave him peppermint-water and prayed for the doctor's return.

But the doctor returned in a rage the like of which the Sagers had never before seen. It was the righteous wrath of a naturally sweet-tempered man. He had discovered the burr and he had observed that the halter-rope had been cut. He also had recalled seeing John disappear around the wagon and return.

All this he shouted before he had dismounted. He said much more as he approached John, and he continued to hurl strange German epithets as he suddenly sat down on an overturned tub on which Mrs. Sager had been sitting, jerked the boy across his knee, and administered an old-fashioned spanking. Then, leading his tired horse, he stalked away, leaving John in tears of anger and weakness.

To John, the worst part of the affair was that his father and mother showed not the slightest appreciation of what he had done for them. Instead, when the next morning dawned and the doctor did not appear, and the Sagers' wagon, for lack of a driver, was left behind by the rest of the company, even John's mother turned against him. He took refuge in sulking as usual and lay all day under the wagon, thankful that there was no work required of him, no matter how it had come about.

Captain Shaw would not have permitted his company to move on without the Sagers had it not been for two reasons. One was that there was no danger from Indians in the South Pass, and the other was that starvation was actually upon the immigrants and he dared not hold them back even one day from Big Sandy Creek, where they hoped to find food. There had been no buffalo for many days. Everyone was hungry. The Sagers themselves had but one meal a day, consisting of fried dough and the tiny

pail of milk one of the poor cows was still able to
contribute to the menu.

So all that day the Sagers camped on the crest
of South Pass, as lonely as the eagles that soared
overhead. But, observe the strange, obstinate luck
that attended John on this journey. Late that afternoon, his father felt stronger, freed as he had been
for twenty-four hours from the dreadful jolting of
the wagon. He sat up and drank a little milk and
even cleaned his gun. And just as he finished cleaning it, there came from the rocks to the north a
thunder of hoofs, and a bull buffalo, followed by a
half a dozen cows, dashed behind the wagon and
disappeared up a little canyon.

With a sudden shout, Henry Sager rammed a
charge into his gun, scrambled somehow into his
saddle, and was off up the canyon. A little later they
heard him shooting. When he came back, the car-
cass of a cow buffalo was dragging at the end of
his lariat.

"I got another one," he said breathlessly. "I'll
drag that in, too."

"Have you the strength?" cried Mrs. Sager. "Oh,
Henry, I'm afraid for you for fear you'll start bleed-
ing again."

But he laughed at her fears and turned his horse
back into the canyon.

Somehow, with everyone except three-year-old

Matilda working, they managed that night to butcher the two buffalo and pack them away. Undoubtedly, they were helped by the steaks they devoured; that is, all but Henry Sager. For him, Mrs. Sager made a great kettle of broth, of which he drank freely.

John did his share in triumphant silence. Once more, he had saved the family. If Kit Carson had been there, he told himself, the scout would have seen that he had full credit for his work! So he was at peace with the world when his father told him to try to start the wagon onward at dawn.

"We've got enough meat to help out the Shaws," said Henry Sager, "and plenty to carry us through a month if we can dry some of it each night. So push along, son."

So sunrise found John guiding the team toward the valley of the Big Sandy, which emptied into the Green River. It was three days later that they overtook Captain Shaw's company, or rather what was left of it. For after leaving South Pass, the caravan, driven by hunger, began to break up, different groups of wagons striking out for themselves. Less than a dozen families were left in Captain Shaw's section when the Sagers' wagon rolled into camp.

Aunt Sally came over, at once, to inquire for Henry Sager's state of health. He was, in fact, very ill again, but he would not allow the good-hearted woman to spend any time over him.

"Lift that blanket off those three tubs, Aunt Sally," he said weakly, "and call the neighbors in."

Aunt Sally looked at the piles of beef, shrieked, and called her husband. The tubs were lifted to the ground, and at Captain Shaw's shout, fifty people gathered, laughing and half crying with joy. That night, for the first time in many weary days, not one of the outfit went to bed hungry.

It was after everyone had eaten his fill that a bulky form appeared in the circle of the Sagers' camp-fire.

"I haf eaten your meat," boomed a big familiar voice, "I must make my thanks."

"O thank God!" exclaimed Mrs. Sager. "Doctor, come and see if you can do anything for my husband!"

"Vhat! He is not vell yet? Sure, I see him and cure him, too, if only he do vhat I say."

He clambered into the wagon, but he came out shaking his head. Many in the caravan had died in the past week. He did not like the look of Henry Sager at all.

# CHAPTER IV

# Fort Bridger

Two days after this the immigrants reached and crossed the Green River. And after making the crossing, though it was only noon, the company went into camp. The reason for this intimately concerned John. Each day found Henry Sager weaker from pain and loss of blood, for this was dysentery in its worst form. He was delirious a good part of the time. It must have been a terrible thing for young Catherine, whose leg was not knitting properly, to lie in the wagon, hour after hour, day after day, and watch and hear her father in his illness. Even John felt that somehow this was hard for her.

At noon, after all had crossed the river and the midday meal was being prepared, Captain Shaw— Uncle Billy, as the children had begun to call him— came to inquire how Henry Sager had come through the ordeal of fording the river.

"He's in very bad shape," said Mrs. Sager, who was feeding the children with hands that trembled from weariness and anxiety.

Uncle Billy climbed into the wagon. Catherine was trying to stifle sobs; and beyond her, her father, thin fingers clasped over his eyes, was sobbing, too. Uncle Billy rubbed his gray-bearded chin anxiously, and, stooping, took one of the sick man's hands.

"Don't give way, Henry! Don't!" he exclaimed.

Henry Sager tried to focus his eyes on Uncle Billy's face. But he was too weak. "Captain," he whispered feebly, "I'm dying . . . and what will become . . . of my wife . . . and all these children? Naomi was . . . right. We should have stayed in Missouri."

"Don't you worry about your family, Henry. Sally and I will look after them. The children are big enough to help a lot. You just put your mind on getting well." Uncle Billy smiled at poor little Catherine, huddled against the tail-board, her leg sticking stiffly before her.

"John," murmured Henry, "needs some man . . . to boss him. . . . Good stuff but needs hard . . . discipline."

"He'll git it!" Uncle Billy nodded as if the thought were not unpleasant. "Dr. Dutch and me, between us, will make him step lively."

But the sick man was not heeding. His eyes were closed. After a moment, Uncle Billy released his hand and put his ear to Henry's heart. Then he looked at Catherine.

"How'd you like to have Uncle Billy and Dr. Dutch lift you out on the ground for a while?" he whispered.

Catherine's blue eyes, swollen from weeping, suddenly brightened. "I want it more than anything!" she whispered.

Uncle Billy slipped out the front end of the wagon to avoid Mrs. Sager's questions, and a moment later returned with the doctor. Mrs. Sager ran toward them as they appeared carrying Catherine between them.

"What are you doing!" she cried, clasping her hands in terrible suspicion.

The two men settled Catherine on a blanket and then Dr. Dutch laid a great, kindly hand on Mrs. Sager's shoulder. "Your good man—" he began huskily.

But he needed to say no more. She broke from

him and ran to the wagon, knowing as she ran that
Henry had gone.

Just before sunset that evening, in a coffin made
from the hollow trunks of cottonwood trees, Henry
Sager was buried beside the Green River. And
Naomi Sager, opening the big Bible, wrote opposite
the entry: *"Born, July 20, 1844, a daughter, Anna."*
Another line: *Died, August 20, 1844, Henry Sager,
aged thirty-eight years."*

The next morning at dawn John started the oxen
on after the other teams.

He had wept most of the night, hiding down by
the rushing water of the river where none might
hear his sobs. All his father's harshness was forgotten. All his own resentful thoughts were as
though they never had been. He only remembered
that from now on he was unprotected, unprovided
for, save what little his delicate mother could do.
Nor were his tears wholly selfish. John wept for his
father's broken dream. Never, never would the farm
on the Willamette yield to his father's plow. Never
would his father rescue from the British the thousand acres of rich black soil of which he had talked
since John's babyhood. It was unbearable to think
of this awful defeat of his father's lifelong hopes.

Toward daylight he had slept, shivering, in the
sands. His mother called him just as the first pale
light touched the top of the western ranges. She

had kindled the fire and was standing over it warming her hands. As John neared the blaze, she looked at him with trembling lips and uttered the one reproach she was to give him—a reproach that was to haunt him as long as he lived.

"John, I wish you'd been a better son to your father, these last few months," she said.

He gulped and stood staring at her, but, strangely for John, without the old sullen resentment. For the first time, it occurred to him to wonder if it had all been his father's fault. He did not reply to his mother, but he actually went ahead with his father's chores without being told. And as he tramped through the dust, that day, beside the oxen, he turned his mother's reproach over in his mind many times. He asked himself what Kit Carson would have said had Kit known how often he had sneaked out of his chores. Supposing, for instance, Kit had come into the camp that evening on the Platte when he had stood watching his mother bring in the baskets of buffalo chips and had heard him all but refuse to fetch the pail of water.

A purplish sort of red crept from the base of John's throat up to his hat-brim. He jerked his head and cleared his throat. "No use thinking about that," he muttered. "Better get my mind on what we all are going to do now Father's—" He gave a

quick sob, then with a loud, "Haw!" he cracked his
whip over the flanks of the oxen.

What the Sagers were going to do was the subject
of many anxious conferences between Mrs. Sager
and the Shaws, with many of the neighbors joining
in. Indeed, the matter concerned the whole company, for with the head of the family gone, the
Sagers would be dependent for food and protection
upon the thirty or forty men remaining with the
captain. And everyone was on starvation rations
now! Dr. Dutch offered to take charge of the outfit
for Mrs. Sager, but as tactfully as she could she
refused. The doctor was a huge eater and no hand
with a gun. The consensus of opinion was that the
family had better travel on to the next safe stopping-
place, the British trading-post, Fort Hall, in what is
now eastern Idaho. There, if possible, Mrs. Sager
would make arrangements to spend the winter, and
in the spring join the first convoy of traders going
to St. Louis. From St. Louis she could return to her
relatives in Ohio.

The decision was a vast relief to Naomi Sager.
She had not the physical strength for pioneering.
As long as her husband lived, his understanding of
this and his wonderful care of her had made it possible to go on. But without him, a future in Oregon
would kill her.

John heard the decision without comment but

with a great sinking of his heart. He wanted to go on to Oregon. He wanted his mother to homestead the thousand acres in his father's name. He was sure that he and Francis, working together, could accomplish as much as their father. But he said nothing, because after the first shock of disappointment, what he felt was a great thought came to him. Kit Carson was at Fort Hall. He would get the scout to beguile his mother into carrying out his father's plans! He rested securely in this thought for many days.

The company worked south along the Green River till it reached what was called the "Rendezvous." This was the spot where hundreds of fur-traders, trappers and Indians met every year to trade with one another. The "Rendezvous" was located on Green River at a point where the gigantic red and purple cliffs that bordered it gave space to some meadow-like flats where grazing and firewood were plentiful. Here Captain Shaw hoped to find sufficient food to put the company on its feet. But once more he was doomed to disappointment.

It was growing late in the year. At this elevation of five thousand feet the nights were biting cold, and the trappers, Indians and white, were leaving the "Rendezvous" to set their trap-lines for the winter. Most of the log huts in which the white men camped were deserted. All of the Indians were gone.

The immigrants were able to buy only a meager supply of flour and jerked beef. But though the Sagers did almost no trading in food, John came rushing into camp late one afternoon, his tanned cheeks burning with excitement.

His mother, with the baby and little Matilda, was calling on Aunt Sally. Catherine was seated disconsolately in the wagon, as usual, watching Elizabeth and Louisa playing at Indians with Francis.

"Catherine!" exclaimed John. "Let me fix you up so's you can move around camp!"

Catherine looked at her brother with lack-luster eyes. "Dr. Dutch said if I moved I'd be crippled for life," she said.

"And I heard Uncle Billy tell Aunt Sally last night that Dr. Dutch was a fool and a horse-doctor," replied John. "And he said if you was his child he'd have you up on a crutch, splint or no splint. And when I told Mother she said she thought so, too, but she didn't dare. But I dare!"

"But it ain't your leg!" retorted Catherine.

"But now look, Catherine. Your leg's held up firm by the splints. What's to prevent me fixing you a sling for that leg, tied around your waist, just like they tie a sling for an arm around the neck. Then you can hop around on a pair of crutches."

"Where'd I get the crutches?" demanded Catherine.

"Ha! Ha! That's where your wonderful brother comes in!" cried John. "See what I found in one of the rubbish-heaps this here 'Rendezvous' is covered with. Some fellow was killed or got cured; anyhow, he threw his crutches away."

He disappeared for a moment around the wagon and returned with a pair of crutches, whittled with real skill from oak.

"A half-breed claimed somebody had given them to him," John explained, looking at his trophies proudly, "and I had to give him my hunting-knife to shut him up. But ain't these fine, old lady?"

Daring and fear struggled in Catherine's thin little face. The six weeks' confinement in the wagon had worn fearfully on the child. "O John! Dast I? Aren't they beautiful! But they're too big."

"The ax will fix that easy enough. Just you let me fix that sling and you stand up, leaning on Francis, and I'll measure and cut them. Come on! Let's do it before Mother comes. And you can hop over to Aunt Sally's. Gosh! Everybody will have a fit and it'll be too late to do anything."

"Yes, come on, Catherine!" cried Francis. "Lean on me."

"No! Lean on me!" squeaked small Louisa. She was so large for her five years and Elizabeth so small for her seven that most people thought they were twins.

"That's right, girls," ordered John. "You tease Catherine to have sense, while I get the sling."

He dived into the horsehair trunk and brought up a roller-towel of stout, unbleached linen. The other three tugged and teased; and finally, half crying and trembling violently, Catherine swung her legs over the lowered tail-board and slid to the ground, where she clung to Francis. John buckled his own belt round the little girl's waist, carefully adjusted her bent leg in one loop of the towel and pulled the other through the belt until the injured leg was fully supported. Then he pinned the towel round the leather with a nail. It required but a moment to measure the crutches and shorten them with the ax.

Catherine balanced on them a moment, timidly, then with a giggle she swung herself forward.

"Francis," ordered John, "you go on her right and I'll be on her left, so she can't fall. Now, head for Aunt Sally's, old lady."

Thus, the little procession proceeded to the Shaws' wagon. The children were greeted with shrieks from their mother and Aunt Sally, with a shout of laughter from Uncle Billy, and the roar of an order from Dr. Dutch.

"Carry her back! She vill be lame for life!"

But when the doctor stepped forward to carry out his threat, John caught his arm.

"You leave her be, Doctor! She'd rather be lame than sit in that old wagon another day, hadn't you, Catherine?"

"Yes, I had!" replied Catherine, who, having made the break, was prepared to fight for her freedom.

"But, Catherine," protested Mrs. Sager gently, "the doctor knows best."

Uncle Billy started to speak, but Aunt Sally laid her hand on his arm. "See if the children can't settle it," she whispered.

"I don't think he knows putty!" cried John. "Anybody knows a broken bone mends itself in six weeks! And, what's more, all the old trappers round here say meat's the worst thing for dysentery. If Dr. Dutch hadn't let my father eat meat, he might be alive today!"

The big doctor, his blond mustache working violently as his lips twitched with anger, seized John by the ear.

"Take your hand off'n me!" cried John. "I'm the head of our home now. I'm doing all my father's work and doing it good, too. You can't lick me again. Nobody can."

"That's true, Dr. Dutch," said John's mother. "He's doing a man's job. I haven't had a bit of trouble with him since his father died."

Reluctantly the doctor released his hold. "Very

vell! But you should not, if he is such a man, permit him to say things I vould knock down a real man
for. See you that?"

"I'm not trying to sass you, Doctor," protested
John, taking a hitch at his breeches, which missed
the support of his leather belt. "I'm just telling you
things for your own good. And I'm going to add
another thing. 'Tain't a mite of use for you to plan
to marry my mother, 'cause I won't let you. Come
on, Catherine and Francis!" And before the grown
people had recovered from their shocked surprise,
the three children had hurried away.

Dr. Dutch clutched his curly yellow hair with
both hands. "Dis is not to be borne! And all you
stand there mit not von vort!"

"Licking won't help John now," said the captain.
"He's reached the age where any boy should be
shut in a barrel for two years and educated through
its bung-hole. I suppose he's had a thousand lickings
in his life, and look at him!"

"I think he's coming out fine!" declared Aunt
Sally.

"I know he is," agreed Mrs. Sager. "I'm terribly
ashamed of the things he said to you, Doctor, and I
do apologize for him."

The anger that stiffened the doctor's face relaxed
sufficiently for a moment for him to give John's
mother a very kindly glance. "I cannot lay it up

against you, dear friend," he said. "But your son,"
his face hardening, "I shall not forgif."

"Shucks, Doctor! He's nothing but a brat! Some
day we may all be proud of him," protested Captain
Shaw. "Stay and have supper with us. Mother has
promised me fried dough and buffalo marrow."

The doctor sighed, then smiled broadly. "Indeed,
my heart does lif in my stomach. I'll stay most glad."

"Mercy, it's almost dark!" exclaimed Mrs. Sager.
"I must go feed my brood!"

But though she allowed him to have his way
with regard to Catherine and the crutches, Mrs.
Sager took John to task in her gentle manner, after
the children had gone to bed. It was too cold to
keep warm before the meager fire, but she detained
him with a hand on his shoulder as he was hurrying
off to his blankets.

"I was very much ashamed, John, of the way you
spoke to Dr. Dutch. I apologized for you."

John was as tall as his mother now. He stood looking levelly into her face, with the firelight flickering
on his eyes that were so like his father's.

"I wouldn't apologize to him in a hundred years.
All I said was true."

"Supposing," said his mother, "that Francis should
say to you, 'John, you use bad grammar. Your teeth
are dirty, and you are a fool when it comes to attending to business matters.' What would you say?"

"I'd knock his head off," answered John promptly.

"But if he said that, it would be absolutely true, John."

"I don't care, I wouldn't let a kid like him say such things to me!" cried the boy. "He'd have no business saying them."

His mother smiled. "That's exactly what Dr. Dutch feels about you."

John blinked. "Oh!" he said abruptly. He shuffled his moccasins in the ashes. "Can I go to bed now?" he asked.

"In a moment, John. Dear, if anything should happen to me, I want you to remember just one thing. Do unto others as you would have others do unto you. I don't know anyone in the world who needs that text quite so much as you do, my son."

John grunted and turned hastily to his blankets. They left the "Rendezvous" the following morning, turning to the southwest toward Fort Bridger, a trading-post owned by the well-known trader and guide, Jim Bridger. The sanitary conditions at the "Rendezvous" had been unspeakably bad, and a day or so after leaving there, Mrs. Sager, who already had a heavy cold, went to bed with an attack of dysentery. John, who had stood up so valiantly to the doctor when there was no sickness in the family, was meekly obedient when Aunt Sally told him to call Dr. Dutch. The doctor came at once, full of kindness toward everyone but John. John watched him jealously. The boy's instincts told him correctly enough that the German doctor would gladly marry his mother. In his heart of hearts, John knew that that might be a wise thing for his mother to do. Nevertheless, he was determined to fight the doctor with every means of which he could think.

Fort Bridger, a little log building on Black Fork Creek, yielded a scant supply of flour and bacon to the immigrants. Scattered sections of the caravan which had gone through a few days before had taken all Jim Bridger would sell. The guide, decently enough, had insisted on saving a share of the supplies for Captain Shaw's section.

Some of the people in the section thought that Mrs. Sager had better stay at Fort Bridger until she felt better. But this she feverishly refused to do, although Jim's wife begged her to stay. Mrs. Sager—indeed, all the immigrants—had been hearing a great deal about the trading-posts of the Hudson's Bay Company. The American traders and trappers were jealous of this British concern, but they admitted that the British could get along with Indians better than Americans and that their trading-posts, compared with the American posts, were models of comfort and good management. Mrs. Sager had firm faith that if she could reach Fort Hall the worst of her troubles would be ended. She swapped Henry's saddle-horse for a tiny supply of flour and bacon, and John urged the tired oxen out from the little valley of the Black Fork, with its border of quivering aspen and its carpet of grease-wood and sagebrush, up through the lavender hills that lay to the west, with the snow-capped peaks of purple mountains beyond.

Two days after leaving Fort Bridger, the night camp was made on a little creek that rushed through a crack in the sloping red floor of a valley that was set with blue spruce. And from the valley, which lay at an elevation of seven thousand feet, one saw the Bear River Divide, the last range that lay be-tween the immigrants and Fort Hall.

The day's travel had been vicious—very cold, and dust, hub-deep, dust everywhere, powder-fine and filled with alkali so that every breath stung nose and throat. Mrs. Sager coughed feebly all day long. Dr. Dutch said that she had lung fever. He never had heard of pneumonia. During the noon halt, she asked the doctor to go out of the wagon and send John in to her. He crept in, his red shirt a deep orange under its coating of dust, his blue eyes very bright and startled in his dust-grimed face. His mother was almost beyond speech.

"I never saw . . . you . . . take little Anna . . . in your arms," she panted.

"There was always plenty to take care of her," he mumbled. "I'll carry her now if you want me to. She's out with Catherine."

"I give her . . . to . . . you. She's your special baby. Keep the children . . . together. . . . Call . . . the doctor."

But not Dr. Dutch nor Aunt Sally nor any of the entreating children could keep Naomi Sager from joining her husband. And that night, in the lonely, high-set valley, silver-powdered with frost in the moonlight, they lined a grave with spruce, wrapped Naomi in the patchwork quilt she had pieced as a child at her mother's knee in Ohio, and laid her in it.

Sixty years later, Catherine Sager wrote for a neighbor in Oregon an account of the death of her father and mother. And, after all that lapse of time, she remembered every detail of their dying moments. But I shall not put those details into this story of John's work. They hurt one too much. And, after all, what we are interested in is not these heart-breaking deaths themselves, but in their effect on the boy, John Sager.

There could be no pause for mourning. That night, after the funeral services, and after the Shaws and the other kindly neighbors had returned to their own wagons, John threw fresh spruce on the fire and sternly ordered Francis and the girls to stop crying. He wiped his own wet cheeks on his sleeve.

"The folks want to divide us up," he said, "one of us to each wagon. She—she told me to keep the children together. And we're goin' to stick together. See?"

"You bet we are!" nodded Francis.

"How about it, Catherine?" John said to the sad little figure on crutches.

"Aunt Sally wants to keep baby Anna," choked Catherine, "but I don't want her to."

"Nor she ain't goin' to," exclaimed John. "Dr. Dutch can show us how to take care of her. Mo— she told me Anna was my own child, and she's goin' to be."

The other children stared at him speechless. *John, who seemed to have hated the baby ever since her arrival, to claim her as his own!* Catherine, in her faded red calico dress; the "twins," in dirty pinafores, their blue eyes still tear-brimmed; little three-year-old Matilda, wrapped in an old knit neck-scarf, clinging to Catherine's skirt; red-headed Francis, in an out-grown blue flannel roundabout coat of John's —all of these eyed him wonderingly and a little wistfully. He was their one hope, the only person to whom they could naturally look for help and guidance, yet it never occurred to them to look to him for these things. Hitherto, John had been to them only a teasing bully, whose occasional kindlinesses were always blotted out by some boyish meanness or brutality.

But John was quite unconscious of the state of the children's feelings. His mind was terribly confused, but he had one or two perfectly clear ideas, and these he proceeded to give.

"Now, I'm the head of the family. I can lick any of you kids, and you know it. If you don't mind what I say—" He paused.

"Huh!" snarled Francis. "I'll obey you just about the way you used to obey poor Mother."

"You dry up!" shouted John. "I don't pretend I was perfect. I'd—I'd give a million dollars to be able to mind her now. And you kids weren't so much better than me, anyhow."

"I ain't goin' to be bullied," insisted Francis. "If you're fair, I'll let you boss. If you ain't fair, I'll let you scalp me before I'll mind."

Catherine spoke quietly. "If you're keeping us up to hear you boys fight, I don't think much of your bossing, John. Francis, you know the last thing Mother said was for us to help John. Keep quiet, do, and let's hear what he wants."

"The first thing is this," said John. "I gotta write down about her in the big Bible. While I'm doing that I want to change the baby's name. I want to call her Henrietta Naomi."

There was a moment's silence; then Catherine nodded with a little aching sob, and Francis said in a husky voice, "I'll fetch the ink."

So, crouched beside the blaze, the children stooping over him, John scratched out "*Anna*" and wrote above it, "*Henrietta Naomi.*" Then, under his father's death, he wrote his mother's: "*Naomi Sager, died September 1, 1844, aged 32 years.*"

# CHAPTER V

# Captain Grant

AUNT SALLY refused flat-footedly, the next day, to give up little Henrietta Naomi. At first she tried to reason with John, but when she had exhausted her breath trying to make him understand that no boy of thirteen could hope to give proper care to a baby six weeks old, she lost her usual sweet temper.

"I declare, John Sager!" she cried. "You are as persistent as a leech! You get back to your oxen now, before Francis upsets the wagon, and leave me and the baby be. Git out! I mean it!"

"She gave her to me!" repeated John for the twentieth time, eying the little flannel-wrapped bundle in Aunt Sally's lap.

He had climbed up on the front seat of the Shaws' wagon so that he and Aunt Sally could hear each other above the rattle of the outfit.

"Your mother can't be held to what she said when she was dying," declared Aunt Sally.

"I don't see that you know so much about taking care of her," exclaimed John. "She cries all the time!"

"That's nothing but wind on her little stomach. She'll soon belch it up. Now, get away from me, John. You can't get 'round me like you could your poor mother."

John flushed, and rubbed his ragged moccasin reflectively against the iron frame of the foot-board. He was angry and puzzled, but he hadn't the slightest idea of giving up the struggle for possession of the baby. His impulse was to seize little Henrietta and run, but common sense told him that in order to be permitted to keep the baby he'd have to find an ally among the grown people. He decided to talk this over with Francis and Catherine. To Aunt Sally's astonishment, he suddenly leaped from the wagon.

Catherine was sitting on the front seat of the Sagers' wagon, with her sisters crowded beside her and behind her. Francis was almost indistinguishable in the cloud of dust through which the oxen plodded. There was no hope for sensible talk with either of them until camp was made for the night.

That evening they made camp high up in a mountain pass, with snowflakes sifting lightly down and hissing on the fire of spruce-logs. John had shot a jack-rabbit in the afternoon and Catherine, helped by the "twins," was stirring it while the boys attended to the chores. The rabbit was tough, so supper was late. Just as the children had seated themselves in the tent door, the fire before them, and their tin pans of stew on their knees, little Matilda crying because her fingers were so cold and the gravy was so hot, Dr. Dutch came stamping into the firelight.

Catherine looked up as if frightened.

"Don't worry, liebe Catherine," laughed the doctor. "I do not come to devour your little supper. I come to see if all goes vell mit the little motherless cubs."

He lifted Matilda, dirty as the poor mite was, to his great knee, wiped her nose and her fingers and proceeded to feed the stew to her with the spoon he took out of his pocket-case.

John, watching the kindly German, had a sudden idea. Now that he could no longer fear that the doctor would become his stepfather, why not make a friend of him? Why not ask his help in getting baby Henrietta back from Aunt Sally.

"Doctor!" blurted John. "My mother told me to keep the children together, didn't she? And that baby Henrietta was my own child."

"So she did, poor Johnny! So she did!" The doctor's eyes softened with tears.

"And Aunt Sally Shaw won't give me back the baby!" cried John.

"So? Vell, poor vooman! She vants to give it mother's care," said Dr. Dutch.

"But you could teach me what to do for her! You don't know how well I can mind, when I want to!" John rose in his earnestness and left his stew, to stand before the doctor.

Dr. Dutch looked at him not unkindly but very doubtfully. "No, I don't know that, Johnny." He shook his head. "I—I—vell, I vould need much proof of that."

John stood clenching his teeth. He was not angry. But, for the first time, a realization of what his disobedience was costing him swept over him. For the first time, something very like contempt for that boy who ran amuck near Fort Laramie, that fool of a John Sager, flooded his mind. So John clenched his teeth in his desire to confess to the doctor what he thought of himself. Somehow, he couldn't do that.

"I guess I can give you the proof if you'll give me the chance," John mumbled at last. "You just bring that baby over here and I'll carry it day and night."

The German doctor stared at the boy long and earnestly. The "twins" were nodding over their empty plates, while little Matilda licked the tin plate with a tongue as pink as a kitten's. But Catherine and Francis listened and watched breathlessly as John, this strange John, so like and so unlike their bullying big brother, did battle with his former enemy.

"Now, just vot is your idea, Johnny?" demanded the doctor, at last.

John drew himself very straight, pushed the flapping, snow-laden hat-brim back from his face, and for the first time in his life spoke up like a man.

"Now that my father and mother are dead," he said, "I want to obey everything they ever said to me—now that it's too late."

"Gott in Himmel!" roared Dr. Dutch. "You haf grown up!" He brought his great fist down on the ground beside him. "This I vill do. I vill come lif in your vagon till ve reach Fort Hall and I vill teach you and Catherine how to take care of the baby."

John gave a great sigh. "That fixes Aunt Sally, I'll bet!" and he returned to his stew.

But although Aunt Sally did actually turn the baby over to the doctor, she did it with a remark that caused John constant uneasiness. She said that if there was any kind of law at Fort Hall she was going to have herself made guardian of Henrietta. But during the remainder of the two weeks that elapsed between Fort Bridger and Fort Hall, the baby in every sense belonged to John.

In spite of the fact that, hitherto, he had refused to have anything to do with her, John, as the oldest of a large family, knew not a little about the care of babies. He had taken a great deal of care of Louisa and of Matilda, before the problem of being thirteen years old had overtaken him. He was, the doctor discovered, because of his superior strength, even more skillful than Catherine. The chief task that faced Dr. Dutch was to teach John how to feed the baby. Catherine was too young to take the responsibility of that.

Curious, was it not, for a boy like John to be tying himself of his own accord to work that any boy of that day or this would declare was fit for girls alone? Or was it curious when you consider what John had been through since that day in April on which Henry Sager wheeled the covered wagon into Captain Shaw's section on the Missouri prairie?

The baby, of course, was dependent on cow's milk, and poor Betsy, the one cow that remained to the Sagers out of the six with which they had left Missouri, could not be expected to average fifteen miles a day of hard traveling and give a good supply of milk. It was all strange to Betsy. She was starving, much of the time, and when the pangs of hunger were worst she was apt to devour anything green in sight, so that every few days her milk would be tainted by some strange herb and tiny Henrietta would be ill.

Dr. Dutch taught John how to add warm water to the milk so that it would not, he said, be too strong for her little stomach. He showed him how to add a few drops of peppermint essence and soda to hot water for the little thing when she writhed and screamed with colic. In the cold weather which now prevailed most of the day in this mountainous country, a daily bath for the baby was not thought of, but on Sundays, with blanket screens rigged up on either side of the tent opening and a fire before it, the doctor showed John how to bathe and dry Henrietta with astonishing speed.

Catherine was a little jealous of John in his capacity of baby's nurse, but the poor child had her hands so full with the "twins" and Matilda and with the cooking, that she had scant time to indulge herself in envy of anyone else's job.

They reached the high valley formed by the joining of the Port Neuf with the Snake River, late on a September afternoon, with the mercury near the freezing-point and a brilliant sunset glorifying the whitewashed walls of Fort Hall which was set on the green floor of the valley. It was dusk when the wagons went into camp within a stone's throw of the twelve-foot log stockade that surrounded the fort.

All day John had urged the oxen on to do their wretched best, with a lightness of heart he had not felt since his father's death. Fort Hall was the stopping-place of Kit Carson, and more than ever Kit Carson represented to John something bigger and finer than a human being. After the other children were asleep, John slipped from his blankets and stole toward the gates of the fort. It was still early in the evening and the gates were wide open, with Indians, traders and immigrants strolling in and out. There was no moon, but the stars were brilliant, and many lights shone from the low buildings that surrounded the circular inner court.

John followed a group of immigrants to a building on the left and entered with them. This was the trading-store. A long counter ran down the center of the room, behind which stood a couple of white men clad in black suits with brass buttons. They looked almost as neat and well dressed as soldiers and were a great contrast to the ragged, unkempt immigrants and the filthy, blanketed Indians. One of the immigrants, Adam Polk, was trying to persuade a clerk to lower the price on powder and shot.

"You all must charge a hundred per cent on what these goods cost you!" cried Polk.

"Depends, sir, on how you estimate cost," replied the clerk courteously. "If you estimate on the London cost, that's one thing. But if you add to the London cost the expense of shipping round Cape Horn to Fort Vancouver, from Fort Vancouver here, which includes two hundred miles by bateaux on the Columbia and six hundred miles by horse pack—"

"Well, I can't afford it, anyhow," interrupted Adam Polk. "I thought maybe it would be cheaper to buy more ammunition and shoot my food than to buy food direct. But I can see you all gouge us either way."

"We didn't set up business to supply immigrants, sir," said the clerk. "We are sent out here to trade for furs. Anything we do for immigrants we do as a matter of accommodation to them. We prefer to keep our goods for the fur trade."

"You can do just that very thing as far as I'm concerned," grunted Polk.

"Sorry, sir." The clerk gave him a not unfriendly smile. "Why, may I ask, do you choose to go on where food is so difficult to obtain? Why not turn south into California? There's an easy trail and a land flowing with plenty. You'll not be able to push your wagons through to the Columbia, you know."

"Dr. Whitman pushed two hundred wagons through last year," said Adam Polk.

"Have you had any talk with the men who were in that outfit?" asked the clerk, darkly. "Let me tell you, friend, that none of them would try it again."

"Yes, but they got their wagons through!" drawled a familiar voice.

John's heart leaped to his throat. He whirled on his heel. A slender figure in a wonderful beaded buckskin coat was moving deliberately up to the counter.

"Now, Carson," protested the clerk, "you know all about guiding a military man like Lieutenant Frémont, but I doubt your ability to give advice to a convoy containing women and children and heaven knows how many of these covered wagons. They must be as hard to drive over these trails as a full-rigged vessel would be."

John began to edge through the crowd until he had reached the scout's side. Carson's slow drawl was giving answer to the Hudson's Bay Company man's protest.

"Last year Lieutenant Frémont took us through country that makes the Snake River Valley look like a race-course and we carried with us—"

Here John twitched his sleeve and Carson looked around. A slow smile softened his keen eyes, his firm lips. "Well, if here isn't young Sager! How are you, boy? Still heading for the Willamette?"

"I'd like to be!" grinned John.

"How's your ma and pa?" asked Carson.

John's face turned scarlet. "They both died, back yonder!" he said huskily.

"Caramba!" ejaculated Carson. "I hadn't heard. Just in from the Salt Lake country. Here, I must learn more about this." His slender, sinewy hand was on John's shoulder. "McGregor," to the clerk, "got any candy in your fly-specked, moth-bitten stock?"

The clerk laughed. "Some hoarhound drops, Kit! That's right, my lad, take him out of here. He talks too much."

With a little parcel of candy in his pocket, John followed the scout out into the starlight.

"I've got a little camp on the far side of the fort," said Carson. "Too noisy near the gates. Hungry?"

"No, sir," replied John, striding along beside his friend.

"That's good, for I suppose it means that food supplies have held up well in your outfit."

"No, food supplies are bad, Mr. Carson," said John, falling into the little trap. "They began to give out after we left Fort Laramie. After South Pass, it got so bad the main caravan broke up and I guess it was mostly everyone for himself. We heard at Fort Bridger that a lot of the folks were going to California because they were afraid they'd starve to death on the Snake River trail."

"And who are you traveling with?" asked the scout, leading John up to a little tent where a fire smoldered before the opening.

"Oh, with Captain Shaw! About a dozen wagons stuck to him. That man, Adam Polk, in the store is one of them."

Carson carefully replenished his fire—a good plainsman is always thrifty with fire-wood—and stood two ribs of beef up to grill in the ashes.

"You may not be hungry, boy, but I am," he said. "Now sit down there and tell me what happened."

John sat before the fire, his hands clasping his knees, his clear eyes on the scout's face, so ruddy in the firelight, and with only an occasional break in his voice told the sad little story. Carson made no pretense that he was not deeply moved. His lips trembled and he wiped his eyes on a brilliant red and blue handkerchief. John told the facts quickly and did not trim them with many details. When he had finished, the scout turned the hissing beef-ribs, cleared his throat and said:

"What are you going to do with the children, John?"

"Well, my mother planned to stay here till spring, then take us all back to St. Louis with some trader's outfit. The Shaws have sort of taken charge of us now. They want to keep the baby and maybe Matilda, and send the rest of us back. Do you think the Hudson's Bay Company would want a gang of kids around here all winter?"

"I don't know," replied Carson. "I do know it's no place for three little white girls. The Hudson's Bay factor, Captain Grant, is a mighty fine man and his clerks are good men. But there are no women but squaws. Still, if Grant will permit it, I don't see what else is to be done."

"Will you be here?" asked John eagerly.

"No, boy; I don't know where I'll be. I'm looking for a man."

"What kind of a man? A bad man? Can I help you? Tell me what he looks like, and if you want me to, I'll shoot him on sight." John looked around him fiercely.

"That's not good talk at all," exclaimed the scout. "You don't shoot anybody on sight, except an Injun or a fellow that you know is going to shoot you." He twirled the beef again and John's mouth began to water. It had been weeks since he had had a full meal. "Here's your rib, boy. Let's see you tuck it behind your heart."

There was silence for a few moments, then Carson asked, "Have you any ideas of your own, John? Do you want to go back to Ohio?"

"No, sir, you bet I don't! I want to take the children on to the Willamette Valley and take up a homestead there just like my father planned. I know Francis and me could soon do as much plowing and planting as Father."

"I believe you and Francis might get there, traveling with some outfit, but, John, you'd never get the girls and the wagon there. That's a job for at least two full-grown men. You heard that talk in the store tonight?"

"Yes, sir, and I've heard lots more like it along the trail. I wouldn't try to take the wagon. I'd travel by pack-train."

Carson shook his head. "You've no idea what it's like, boy! Any trails you've been over so far are nothing compared with the Snake River you'd be following for three hundred miles. If the Shaws could take you on up to the Whitmans' mission, maybe they'd keep you for the winter. But maybe they couldn't. I suppose the immigrants have been swarming on them for weeks, eating them out like locusts. And there's mighty little chance of a fur convoy passing there in the spring to take you all East. I guess, after all, your mother's idea was best. You stay here, this winter."

Disappointment sat on John's heart with sudden crushing weight.

"I thought you'd understand!" he cried. "I've let 'em all talk and talk, because I thought when I found you, you'd help me do what my father

wanted. And, instead, you talk like the rest of them!"
The scout finished his beef and tossed the bone
into the fire. He smiled a little sadly at John.

"I do understand, boy, and I wish I was fixed
so I could help you get up to the Willamette. But
this man I'm looking for—" He paused and studied
John's face. "Look here, boy. I don't want you to
think I'm going back on your hopes of me, for a
little thing. If you can keep a secret, I'll tell you
why I can't let anything turn me aside."

"Certainly, I can!" declared John stoutly.

"I believe you," Carson nodded. "Well, you know,
don't you, that both the United States and England
are hoping to get California away from Spain?"

"Yes, I've heard Father talk a lot about that and
Oregon."

"That's it! Well, there's a Spaniard in California
who runs the whole show for Spain. Lieutenant
Frémont, who was there last year—I was his guide—
is anxious to make friends with this Spanish grandee.
But he hates Americans and won't give 'em a chance
to get close to him. Now, Lieutenant Frémont
learned something about that Spaniard this spring.
He heard that his only daughter had been run off
with by a Spanish half-breed that claims to be the
son of the grandee and a squaw. He heard that the
half-breed was working for the Hudson's Bay Company as a trapper. I'm looking for that half-breed

to see if I can get news of the girl to take to
Lieutenant Frémont, who'll take it to the Spanish
don. See?"

John's eyes were bright. "I see! I understand!
Gee, if I didn't have this other job on my hands,
maybe you'd take me with you."

"I might. You've got the makings of a scout in
you. But things being as they are, I guess you'd
better get your sisters back to Ohio."

John sighed heavily. "Thank you for the meat,
sir, and the candy. It'll be a real treat to the children."

"Tell 'em I'll be 'round to see them in the morning."

John nodded, and plodded off through the starlight toward his own outfit.

The following day was spent by the immigrants
in excited conferences with one another and with
Captain Grant of the Hudson's Bay Company. The
British were much troubled by the great numbers
of American families who were pouring into the
Oregon Country. The ownership of Oregon would
be decided by whichever nationality of citizens was
in the majority in the near future. All the immigrants that Captain Grant could turn from Oregon
to California were just that much loss to the American cause. So Captain Grant appeared at Uncle
Billy Shaw's breakfast fire and began to talk very

seriously with him about the foolhardiness of his
attempting to lead his section over the Snake River
trail and up into the Blue Mountains where winter
was already showing its white face. Shortly the
householders of the other wagons had gathered
round and John hovered on the outskirts, in wordless anxiety.

It was a long time before the council of elders
took up the case of the Sager children. First Captain
Grant told them the names of the families who had
come through within the past few weeks and had
with great good sense decided in favor of California.
Then he told them the names of the families who
had left their wagons in the stockade of Fort Hall
and had foolishly gone on toward Oregon. And he
read from a list in his hand the names from those
of General Gillian's caravan who had been drowned
in the Snake River, had frozen to death in the
wilderness of the Blue Mountains, had died of lung
fever, or had been drowned in the falls of the
Columbia. One family of six had strayed from the
trail, after leaving the Grande Ronde, and had
starved to death, he said.

There was much excited talk after this. Several
men, after consulting with their wives, announced
that they were going to California. The remaining
three or four families decided to leave their wagons

but push on toward the Willamette Valley. Captain
Shaw was the stout champion of these latter.

"Good for you, Polk, and you, Ames, and you,
Arkwright!" he cried, shaking hands with each man
who voted for the Willamette. "We'll give ourselves
a day here to rest our stock and repack, then on we
go!"

Captain Grant stood watching the scene, scowling a little, though secretly he must have been
pleased at the effect he'd had in breaking up the
little group of wagons. John had taken a great dislike, as did many Americans, to the Hudson's Bay
Company factor. He thought he had a cruel, hard
face and that he talked to the Americans as though
they were servants or very stupid children. For just
a moment, as Grant was turning away, John thought
Uncle Billy had decided not to leave them and the
other children at Fort Hall. But not Uncle Billy!

"O Captain Grant!" he cried. "I'd like to arrange
to leave five children, the oldest thirteen, with you
for the winter." He went on to explain the situation
to the factor, drawing him aside as he did so and
beckoning John to draw near. "This is the oldest
child, John Sager. In a way, we're not asking charity.
Their mother turned over to me enough money to
pay for their board during the winter, and their
outfit should be good enough, by spring, to carry
them back to St. Louis."

Captain Grant rubbed his chin. "Can't say I like the idea, sir. This fort is no place for white children and I've no idea when I could be rid of them. We deal with outfits coming from the East far more often than we send outfits east. Green River "Rendezvous" might easily be our limit, next spring."

"I don't want to stay here, Uncle Billy!" protested John.

The factor looked at the tall boy, grimly. "I suppose you're the usual spoiled American cockerel! I warn you that this place is under military discipline and you'll be handled accordingly."

John scowled. "I'm not going to stay where I'm not wanted."

"You'll do what you're told, young fellow," retorted Uncle Billy.

"Come over to my office, Shaw," said Captain Grant, "and I'll see what arrangements I can make."

John turned on his heel and made his way blindly back to his wagon. His last hope had failed him. He took baby Henrietta from Catherine's tired arms and called Francis to him.

"Let's take a little walk, Francis," he said. "I want to talk to you."

They circled, unseeingly, round the fort while John detailed the account of his talk with Kit Carson, the night before, and the arrangements just made by Uncle Billy with Captain Grant.

"Gosh! Isn't that hard luck!" groaned Francis.

"Look here, Francis, do you think we can stand like trees and let our two little sisters be taken away from us? I tell you I can't! Do you think I'm going to let them smash up everything Father wanted to do? Well, I'm not going to let it happen, that's all. If you and Catherine will back me up, I'm going to take you all on to the Willamette."

Francis' bright eyes danced. "Of course, we'll back you! How'll you do it?"

"I haven't got it all worked out yet. We've got to give these folks all the slip, until we're so far out on the Snake River that it will be too late to send us back. My idea is that we'll slip off tonight. That will give us a day's start. We can pack all our things that we'll need on the oxen and lead the cow. Catherine can ride all the time on one of the oxen. Matilda can, too. I guess the rest of us children have walked at least half the thirteen hundred miles between here and Missouri, so we'd ought to be able to do seven or eight hundred more. And we'll be together."

Francis nodded. "You bet! Say, there comes Kit Carson now. Are you going to tell him?"

"No!" exclaimed John. "Not him or anyone but Catherine, and her only about five minutes before we start. Good-morning, Mr. Carson!"

The scout sauntered up. "I was just going to make

my call on you folks. Is that the littlest baby?"
smiling at the tiny face that snuggled against John's
shoulder. "She looks like the Sager tribe, all right.
Let's go see the other sisters."

He played with the younger children for an hour,
then took his leave, after drawing John aside.

"I'm pulling out on the quiet, boy, before daylight. I hope you'll have a good winter here. It's a
great place to learn the fur business, so maybe you'll
profit by it, after all. Here's a little something to
help you out." And he turned away, leaving in
John's hand a ten-dollar gold-piece.

John stared at the money, then made a dash after
the scout. "Mr. Carson! Mr. Carson! Wait a moment."

Carson turned and watched the boy approach.
John was as big as a man and his childish face and
voice were hard to reconcile with his size.

"Mr. Carson!" John took the scout's arm with a
hand that trembled with the excitement of an idea
that had just come to him. "I just can't stay here.
I hate that Captain Grant! He doesn't want us. You
know he doesn't. You take us back as far as Fort
Bridger with you. Captain Bridger's wife wanted
us to stay before, and the captain will take us out
in the spring. He told my mother he would."

The scout stared uneasily at John. Certainly he
did not wish to hamper himself by a wagon load of

youngsters, yet he knew that there was hard common sense in the boy's plea. Fort Hall *was* no place for white children. It *was* a great pity to break up the family. Jim Bridger's wife could give the baby better care at the trading station than Mrs. Shaw could on the Snake River trail.

John, talking rapidly, dragged Carson toward Captain Shaw who was coming out from the stockade.

There followed a long hour of argument. But finally Uncle Billy agreed to the desirability of John's scheme, and the scout gave a reluctant consent to undertaking the job. Only Aunt Sally refused to agree and the men decided to act without her help.

John had now several free hours before him in which to carry out certain items in his scheme which he had mentioned to no one.

That ten-dollar gold-piece spelled not candy and gaudy moccasins to John as the scout had supposed it would. It spelled powder and bullets and pemmican.

Pemmican was not pleasant food to taste, but it was very nourishing. It was much used by trappers, and John, who had first heard of it at the "Rendezvous," had been watching ever since for a chance to buy some or trade for it. But this had not been possible until now. The Hudson's Bay Company

kept a small supply behind the counter. Pemmican
was prepared by the Indian squaws. They dried
the meat of a buffalo, and afterwards pounded it
almost to powder—a powder full of fibers. The hide
of the buffalo was made into a bag. Then the meat
was mixed with melted tallow and the whole poured
into the hide, where it hardened and was supposed
to keep sweet indefinitely.

When Mrs. Sager and the children had tasted
pemmican at the "Rendezvous," they had made dis-
gusted faces and spat it out. They said it tasted
rancid and was full of sand and buffalo-hairs. But
John and Francis, who prided themselves on being
seasoned trail men, ate their share and pronounced
it not bad. At any rate, it was certainly a very valu-
able food for such an expedition as John was preparing for, and he showed good sense when he
planned to expend his gold-piece on that and a
good supply of ammunition.

# CHAPTER VI

# The Wild Scheme

For hours that afternoon John sought to find a moment when no one belonging to Captain Shaw's outfit was in the store. But this was not possible. The men and women of the outfit were struggling to prepare themselves for the worst part of their terrible journey, with very little money with which to meet the very high prices. This required hours of bargaining. Toward sunset John reluctantly turned for help to a half-breed Indian with whom he had scraped an acquaintance during the hours of watching. He led the half-breed outside and showed him the list he had made on a scrap of paper.

"Look here, Jo," he said. "Ten dollars will buy me one of those bags of pemmican in there, five bags of powder and two hundred bullets. I don't want anyone to know I'm buying 'em. What will you charge me to do it for me?"

"Where's the ten dollars?" asked the half-breed eagerly.

"I ain't going to tell you where it is, but I'll tell you who gave it to me. It was my friend, Kit Carson. He's in that store right now, and if you try any deviltry on me, all I've got to do is to tell him. See?"

The half-breed, who was not quite so tall as John, a stocky fellow in a tattered blanket coat, grunted. "What you offer me?"

"I offer you a man's suit of black clothes, a very fine suit. It was my father's and is like new."

"Where is it?" demanded Jo.

"Wait a minute." John hoped the half-breed couldn't see how nervous he was. "I ain't going to give you all that for three minutes' work. I want ten pounds of that jerked venison you told me you had."

"Five!" grunted Jo.

"Ten or nothing!" declared John, much encouraged and pleased by his own nerve. "There are plenty of folks would like that black suit."

"Let's see 'em," said the half-breed.

"Come on, before it's too dark in the wagon," exclaimed John.

Luckily, the children were scattered about the camp, so that Jo was able to make his examination of the suit unobserved. John had no idea how the half-breed's heart yearned and exulted over the broadcloth suit that had been Henry Sager's Sunday suit for fifteen years. This was such a suit as only the chief men of the Hudson's Bay Company wore. A regiment of soldiers could not have kept Jo from doing John's errand. But, like a true trader, he concealed his pleasure.

"I'll do it," he said. "You stay here."

"No, I'll come along to the store and give you the money when you get inside."

"Don't need money till I bring you the goods. My credit's fine. You stay here. You hide that suit. Don't let anyone see it, sabe?"

John nodded, and after the half-breed hurried from the wagon he grinned. The suit was a happy thought, he told himself. Jo really wanted it.

In what seemed an impossibly short time, Jo was back, grunting under the load of supplies. John examined them carefully, then rolled up the black suit.

"Don't you tell where you got this, Jo, or I'll be in trouble and they'll make you give it up."

"Tell nothing!" snorted Jo. "I'm no fool!"

He tucked the suit tenderly under his arm, and then permitted himself to show his tobacco-stained teeth in a grin.

"Good trading!" he said. "You're happy. I'm happy. Maybe some day we'll trade again."

"Look, Jo!" exclaimed John. "They say along the Snake River you trade fish-hooks and tobacco with the Indians for salmon. How can I get fish-hooks and tobacco from the Hudson's Bay Company? I haven't any more money."

Jo looked around the interior of the wagon. John had lighted a candle and the feeble flame flickered on the mahogany bureau, the chairs, the horsehair trunk, the heap of buffalo-skins and blankets, the three guns, and everywhere a mess of children's odds and ends mixed with dishes and other household equipment. Jo pointed to the mirror on top of the bureau.

"You give me that. I'll bring you plenty of fish-hooks and rope tobacco."

"Bring 'em first," said John.

Jo disappeared, returning after a time with a worn deerskin bag from which he produced a mass of fish-hooks and several feet of tobacco. John now was quite at sea. He knew what the price of the two articles was at the Company store. He had no idea what was the value of the mirror. And he dared not prolong the bargaining lest someone come in upon him. He hastily picked out five dozen fish-hooks of various sizes, and measured ten feet of rope tobacco, then looked up questioningly at the half-breed. Jo grunted, took back two feet of the tobacco. John added a dozen fish-hooks to his collection.

Jo thought for a moment, then said, "I'm through!"

"All right, Jo! Good-by!" exclaimed John hastily.

"Good-by," returned Jo, lifting the mirror carefully from the bureau and grinning delightedly at his own ragged reflection therein.

John quickly concealed his newly acquired supplies under a buffalo-pelt and went out to round up his flock of children. He helped Catherine bundle the younger fry off to bed, then he drew her and Francis to the fire. Keeping tight hold of his sister's arm, for fear she might bolt and give him away to the Shaws, he told them of his plans, in a husky whisper.

Catherine, her thin little face dirty, her eyes enormous under her wild mass of hair, did not make a sound for a full moment after John had ceased speaking. Then she whispered:

"Then we don't have to give up baby and Matilda! O John, I think you are the best and smartest brother in the world!"

"Sho!" whispered John sheepishly. Then he

looked at Francis and said, "Say, you never can tell about girls, can you!"

Francis shook his head. "We sure thought you'd go tell Aunt Sally, Catherine," he said.

The little girl gave him an indignant look. "You must be crazy! What do we do first, John?" tossing her hair out of her eyes.

"Well," said John, "we'll put on all the warm clothes we've got and we'll carry what extra there are—"

"There won't be any extra," interrupted Catherine. "Most everything's worn out."

"We'll make up the same kind of an outfit the others are talking about," went on John.

"I know, John, see if I don't!" exclaimed Francis.

"Sh-sh! Not so loud!" whispered Catherine.

Francis lowered his voice. "The tent, cooking outfit, two blankets apiece, enough buffalo-hides for beds, all the food we can find, our guns and powder and bullets, the ax— Guess that's all. When shall we pack up, John?"

"I should think we could do most of it now in the wagon," replied John. "We can take turns watching out here, and if anyone comes, the guard will cough. I'll take first turn. You just pack that old carpet-bag with the baby's things. She'll need more than anybody."

Nobody interrupted the children's preparations.

The Sagers, for the first time, were off the minds of
everybody. Aunt Sally and Uncle Billy were spend-
ing the evening with Captain Grant who still hoped
to turn them toward California. Carson had let
Uncle Billy know that he wished to make a very
quiet start, long before dawn, and John had orders
to drive the wagon out to the edge of the camp and
to go to bed with all his packing done.

After everything had been stowed in the wagon,
the three children went sedately around the camp
saying good-by to everyone. This finished, they
moved the wagon out to the spot chosen by Carson
and then, it being nearly nine o'clock, they saw a
light in the Shaws' wagon and trooped over to bid
them farewell.

Aunt Sally broke down and cried and John was
so afraid that Catherine, in order to comfort the
dear soul, would give his scheme away, that he
dragged the little girl off before she had time even
to kiss Aunt Sally. He did not allow her to speak
until he had thrust her into the wagon beside her
sisters.

He and Francis rolled themselves in blankets
under the wagon. Shortly, Francis was asleep but
John lay wide awake quivering with excitement.

It was after ten when he slipped out of his
blankets and went to find Kit Carson. The scout
was seated before his camp fire cleaning his gun.

"I've come to tell you," mumbled John, "that Aunt Sally's going to keep us with her. We aren't going with you, after all."

Carson looked up. The fire was low and he could not see the boy distinctly. John was thinking uneasily that it was only partly a lie, that they would be with the Shaws after a few days alone on the Snake River trail.

"Going to take you all, is she?" exclaimed Carson. "Well, I'm not going to pretend I'm not relieved. It was no job for a bachelor! And that being so, I'll be slipping away before midnight. I've had news that makes me want to get out without anyone's knowing it."

"Good-by, then!" said John. "You've been awful good to us."

"Good-by, boy! You're a good fellow! I'll see you next year, I guess."

John swallowed hard and turned away.

He dared not sleep, therefore he dared not lie down. For an hour he prowled up and down beside his wagon. About twelve he saw Carson's outfit melt away in the starlight. An hour after this young Henrietta Naomi whimpered for her bottle. He had it waiting and popped it into her mouth, and wakened Catherine and Francis.

He really had made his plans remarkably well. The oxen and cow were staked in a bit of meadow about three hundred yards from the wagon. No guard was kept with the camp set so close to the fort. The night before, the three oldest children had dragged all their baggage down to the meadow edge and had hidden it under a pile of sagebrush.

When Catherine and Francis were awakened, John gave the baby to Catherine, Francis picked up Matilda, who did not waken, and John lifted Elizabeth and Louisa to their feet.

"Injuns! Injuns!" he said in an awful whisper. "If you make a sound they'll come out and get you. Come on! We'll run and hide from them!"

It was a pathetic reminder of the terrors of the past months on the trail to see these seven- and five-year-old children waken to utter fear and utter silence. Under the brilliant frosty stars, the five stole through the tall sagebrush to the meadow. Here, somehow, the baggage was tied to the pack-saddles which Henry Sager had made in Missouri. No one had been sure that the wagons could go farther than Fort Hall and most people were supplied with the saddles.

John and Francis, long since, had learned how to load a pack-animal, and though they now were obliged to work by starlight, the job was done sufficiently well for the time being. Catherine, with Matilda and Louisa, was mounted on one ox; Francis, with Elizabeth, on the other. Then, with the cow and oxen tied nose to tail, John, with the baby in his arms, took the lead-rope and started off through the sagebrush, heading due west.

It was a foolish, childish sort of plot. Everything was against its success except that in a country so wild as this all nature plotted with John to confuse and outwit the grown people. A wind-storm rose with the sun and blew the sand over the children's tracks from the meadow to the main trail.

By noon, the younger children had begun to whimper with weariness and cold and John led the animals into a clump of willows on a little creek about a quarter of a mile from the trail. Hardly had they reached this haven when the snow began to fall. John and Francis set up the tent, into which the baby and Matilda were immediately tucked under blankets. They had eaten their breakfast cold, but with willows and falling snow as a screen, they now dared build a rousing fire, and Catherine made a pemmican stew. She held her nose while she ate her share, but the other children devoured theirs without protest. When they could hold no more and the baby refused a second bottle of warm milk, they spread the two buffalo-pelts in the tent and, crowded together for warmth, the seven slept like winter bear cubs until dawn the following day.

During the night the snow had turned to rain, then the clouds had blown away and the sun rose gloriously. In the valley, all was yellow sand and gray-green sagebrush, but the mountains that rose on either hand were clothed in flashing white from top to toe. The cattle had found an abundance of grass in the low ground near the willows. The children were rested and in wonderful spirits. John was proud of his handiwork.

"What do you suppose Uncle Billy and Aunt Sally are doing about now?" asked Catherine at breakfast.

"I don't know anything about them," replied John. "But if that soup is hot, we'd better put the fire out and get started. There's sure to be someone along the trail today, and I want to find a good hiding-place we can camp in till they're all gone by. Then we'll follow. When we've got about a week along, so they can't send us back, we'll walk in on them some night."

The fire was stamped out and Francis brought the cattle up to the tent to receive their loads. They had just adjusted the first pack-saddle when Elizabeth said suddenly:

"I hear something! Maybe it's Injuns!"

"Hush! Sh-sh-sh—" Only children who had lived through deadly fear could be so silent.

Along the rough trail from the northeast came the dim sound of hoofs, the creak of wheels. The children peeked silently from the willow thicket. A line of oxen, twenty of them, laden with packs. Five two-wheeled carts in which women were sitting. Men tramping beside the pack-animals.

"That's Uncle Billy's old Pie Biter at the head of the bunch. You can see him limp clear from here," whispered Francis.

"They don't dream we're watching them," said John, exulting, one grimy hand ready to descend on Matilda's mouth at the first sound.

"Why not stay here another day, John?" asked Francis. "Looks like this was a pretty good hiding-place."

John bit his nails thoughtfully as the little caval-cade disappeared. "That's what we'll do," he said finally. "But any young one I find outside of this clump of willows will get a licking from me. We'll keep the cattle right in here and let 'em pick what grass and bark they can. Say, isn't this Sunday?"

"Yes, it is," replied Catherine. "I remember Aunt Sally said they always read the Prayer-book and sang hymns at the fort on Sunday and it would be just like going to church once more. And when she said it, that was to be day after tomorrow and that was day before yesterday."

"Gosh, Catherine!" groaned Francis. "You can talk more foolishness!"

"This being Sunday, then," declared John, "we're going to have services right here ourselves."

The children stared at him. A little red around

the ears, John went over to the old carpet-bag which contained the baby's things and took out the Bible.

"This is a good way to keep quiet till Uncle Billy's ears is a mile or so away," he said. "Come on, all you folks, squat round."

"I ain't going to do anything of the kind!" exclaimed Francis. "You ain't our father or mother, and they're the only ones in our family I'd let read the Bible to me!"

John was deeply embarrassed. He thoroughly understood Francis' feelings, and in a way sympathized with them, but he was fully determined to make up for the things he'd failed in with his parents. This was one of his ways of making up. His embarrassment showed in a flash of anger.

"You'll listen," he said, "or I'll knock your head off!"

Francis put out his tongue. "I'm *not* a-goin' to listen!" he declared.

John dropped the Bible and seized Francis at the same moment. There was a struggle which ended as usual, with Francis crying into the crook of his arm but sullenly obedient. John, breathing rapidly, opened the Bible and thumbed through it until he found the Twenty-third Psalm, which he read in a very firm voice. He followed this with the first chapter of Genesis. Then he closed the book and silently put it away.

John was very gentle with the children for the rest of the day. He played games with them to keep them quiet, winning even Francis at last to join in a contest of making cat's cradles. They went to bed with the setting of the sun, and were on the trail the next morning before sunrise.

John moved at the head of the little procession, his chest arched in pride. Who could say, he told himself, that he had not managed this business as well as a man? He wondered if the scout should come upon them, would he try to force them all to return to the fort. He concluded that Carson would not be so cruel or so stupid, after seeing what a trail leader John was. "My," he murmured, "I could easy take the young ones through to the Willamette all by myself. Maybe I won't try to catch up with Uncle Billy, just to show everybody!"

It was a beautiful day of sunshine, with the temperature at May heat at noon and freezing as the sun sank at night. They made their evening camp a little beyond the spot occupied the previous night by Uncle Billy's outfit. It had been carefully chosen, with grass for the animals and wood and water for the humans. And more of John's wonderful luck! One of the two-wheeled carts had been abandoned here.

John found the reason for this when he crept down the steep bank of the river for a pail of water.

The remains of an ox lay on the stones near the water's edge. The hoof of a foreleg was still caught in a crevice, with the broken bone telling the story of the accident. The animal had been butchered as he lay and John noted sadly that, between buzzards and other wild visitors, not a shred of meat remained.

But the cart was, John thought, glorious luck. There was no yoke, to be sure, but he and Francis could rig up some sort of rope harness, which, by the light of the fire, that evening, they proceeded to do. Why the wagon had been so easily abandoned did not trouble the children. They had no slightest doubt of their ability to make use of it, for they had no actual knowledge of the sort of trail over which the wagon would have to travel.

# CHAPTER VII

# The Lonely Trail

THEY were entering the valley of the Snake River, which runs east to west across what is now the State of Idaho, then turns northward to empty finally into the Columbia. We must make ourselves a mental picture of this valley in order to understand what were John's difficulties of travel. Imagine a very wide valley with mountains to the south and to the north, all topped with snow. The valley, in a general view, is a high plain broken by little hills and depressions and often covered with masses of broken rock. Cut through the high plain is a mighty canyon or chasm, in which flows the Snake River. The walls of the canyon are not very high in their eastern beginning, but they grow higher and higher, the river flowing deeper and deeper, until in places they are actually a mile high. Into the canyon of the Snake River flow many creeks and brooks, sometimes over smooth-lying beds of sand, near which was good feeding for animals, sometimes flowing over tumbled rocks and falls, so rough that the clumsy oxen would have thirsted to death before they could have reached the leaping waters.

The trail kept in a general way along the crest of the canyon. But only in a general way. So rough, so crossed and recrossed by chasm and upheaved rocks, were the mighty banks of the Snake that the trail twisted and turned oftener than did the river. The diary of one of Captain Shaw's section speaks of crossing the Snake River three times in a single day! Some days, with a good horse outfit, it was possible to make fifteen to twenty miles. Some days, two or three miles. Some days, there was grass for miles on either side of the trail, scattered among enormous growths of sagebrush. Sometimes, for two or three days, there was no grass and the poor dumb brutes starved.

It was over country such as this that the seven children traveled, difficulties such as this that John was facing so boldly. He had heard, as we know, much about these difficulties, but his imagination had been unable to paint them as they were. Such a camp as they made this fourth night was fine enough to lull anyone's anxieties to rest. Even the baby ceased her fretful crying and, except for her midnight feeding, took a full night's sleep.

But they were wakened next morning by rain, a cold rain. Nothing daunted, John thanked his luck once more for the cart and packed the younger children into it under blankets and tent canvas, while he and Francis plodded with the oxen. The trail was an easy one that day, across a sandy flat, for the most part, with only an occasional steep grade up which they had to help push the cart. Again they camped near the traces of Uncle Billy's night's halt, where in the driving rain they hunted eagerly for some souvenirs of the grown folks' forgetfulness or bad luck. But only close-gnawed beef-bones rewarded them.

The next day dawned clear and they made good going until mid-afternoon, when the trail stopped at a low spot in the canyon wall. The river was wide and smooth here, with several little cedar-grown islands in the middle. On the further shore the ruts of the trail could be seen distinctly, lifting up a sandy bluff. The Sagers had crossed countless streams since leaving Missouri, and the two boys had lost all fear of strange and rushing waters.

"How shall we make it, John, ford or float?" asked Francis.

"Only one way to tell," replied John.

He climbed on the back of the meek old cow and Francis pushed her into the stream. In a little over the length of her body, she was swept off her feet and was swimming. John allowed her to follow her instinct, which was to turn back. He was wet to his knees.

"That water's ice-cold," he said, as he slid from the cow beside Francis. "Can't risk getting the baby wet in that."

"I never thought about rivers when we talked over this trip!" exclaimed Catherine, trying to hush the crying baby as she limped up to the boys. She was very lame, but had abandoned her crutches at Fort Hall.

John grunted. "I'd like to camp on one of those islands tonight," he said after a moment. "Looks like they have the only wood round here. We'll do like we did crossing the Green, Francis. Make bushels of this willow weed into bundles, put the cart box on them and raft ourselves over."

"We can't never lift that cart box!" scoffed Francis.

Elizabeth, followed by Louisa, scrambled down the bank. They both began to cry. John looked down at them. They were wrapped in all sorts of odds and ends of little shawls and knitted scarfs. They were dirty and uncombed, yet nothing could fully quench the charm of their curly yellow heads and their mother's sweetness of lips and eyes reflected in their little faces. But no thought of this crossed John's mind as he glared at them.

"Stop sniveling!" he shouted. "Isn't the baby enough?"

He had long since brought the "twins" to complete obedience. They choked back their sobs and stood staring at the river with startled eyes.

"The cart box has all its cracks stopped up," volunteered Catherine.

John nodded. "But it won't float high enough unless we buoy it up like the men always do. Come on, Francis, I'll cut brush and you carry it down the bank."

There was an hour's hard work in tying the great bundles of brush and laying it raft-wise on the river-bank. This done, they backed the cart so that it stood end to end with the raft. John then unhitched the oxen, brought them round and fastened them to a rope tied to the tail-board of the **cart** box.

"Now, Francis," he ordered, "start 'em up in a hurry!"

Francis cracked the whip, the beasts lunged, and the cart box was dragged off the wheels onto the raft beneath, where the boys lashed it fast with grazing-ropes.

"Gosh!" exclaimed Francis, gazing with delight at the clumsy craft. "You really ain't always a fool, John! The oxen can drag her right on into the river, huh?"

John nodded. "Suppose we'll have to make two trips of it. Get the girls over first and come back for the packs. Hurry up, now. It's almost sunset."

The crazy boat or raft, it was a little of both and not much of either, followed the oxen into the water. Francis tied it to a rock, then released the tow-rope and John brought the oxen to shore. The boat rode rather askew but well out of the water, so much so that John dared to load the packs in with the children. Then he hitched the oxen again to the tow-rope, mounted one of the animals and once more plunged into the river.

One can but wonder what Henry and Naomi Sage would have said, could they have looked down from heaven upon that terrible crossing. The grand, desolate valley; the wicked, rushing river; the tiny, tiny, fragile craft with its freight so inexpressibly dear to them. Surely, the sight was

enough to make even one safe in heaven tremble
and weep.

The boat swung downstream at once, so that the
oxen, goaded by John to swim directly across, were
turned by the boat, with their heads upstream and
for a time were actually dragged downstream. Francis, crouching in the end of the boat, tried valiantly
by means of the tent-pole to get some sort of steer-
age way, but this was impossible. The "twins" and
Matilda began to scream, and Francis yelled at them
savagely to be quiet. The maddened and bewildered oxen struggled to turn back to the shore they
had left.

John was frightened for an instant almost into
senselessness. The screams of the children unnerved
him, and for the first time since leaving Fort Hall
his confidence deserted him. For a moment he allowed the oxen to have their own way, and as they
managed to twist themselves toward the shore they
had just quit, he caught sight of the old cow plunging into the water to follow the oxen as she had so
many times before. Instantly, John saw hope.

"Co', bossy! Co', bossy!" he shouted.

Old Betsy swam toward him and he caught her
grazing-rope, at the same time, with all the force
of goad and voice, turning the oxen toward the
island. Instantly, Betsy's extra weight on the boat
told. Slowly, very slowly, the current lost its grip

and the boat began to move, at first so slowly one could hardly see it, then more and more surely, toward its haven.

Just at dusk, John, shivering so that he could scarcely use his hands, fastened the boat to a cedar-tree that leaned over the water and helped the sobbing children ashore. Somehow they gathered twigs and dried needles enough to make a hand-warming fire and then Francis, not exhausted as was John, cut enough wood for a roaring blaze. Once they were warmed, the "twins" and Matilda stopped weeping and Catherine laid the sleeping baby on a bed of pine-needles while she boiled a great kettle of pemmican-stew with which, as a special treat, permitted by John, she served each child a bit of fried dough the size of a walnut.

The animals found wonderful grazing on the island, which was not much bigger than Fort Hall in extent.

"I suppose they think the grass is worth the swim," said Francis, as they sat around the fire after supper and heard the crop, cropping that came so close to their backs.

"How are we going to get the cart-wheels over here?" asked Catherine, suddenly.

"That's right! Takes you to think of something disagreeable!" said John crossly. He was wrapped in a blanket watching his clothes steaming on the rack he had made for them beside the flames. "They can lie there and rot for all of me! I know I'm not going back for them!"

Catherine and Francis looked at each other, helplessly. John saw the look.

"Think I can do everything?" he shouted, furiously.

"I know one thing," declared Catherine, stoutly; "we'll be awful bad off without the cart, specially in stormy weather."

"You'd better go over and get the wheels then, yourself," was John's retort.

Francis yawned.

"You and Catherine go on to bed," was John's next order. "I've got to keep this fire up till my clothes are dry. Nobody to do it for me."

"I'd try, only I'd go to sleep," said Catherine.

John sniffed and turned his shirt round to dry the sleeves, and the other two went into the tent.

The truth is that John was for the first time realizing what the responsibility meant which he had taken on himself. He had thought that he had learned all about responsibility after his father's death, but now he saw that always he had had a grown person—Aunt Sally, Uncle Billy, Dr. Dutch—to lean on. When he had decided to do certain things, it always was with the knowledge in the back of his mind that if it was a foolish decision he probably would be prevented from carrying it out. It now dawned on him that grown people really were better capable of saying what and how important things should be done than was John Sager.

"Gee, thirteen is pretty few years to learn about everything that my father took thirty-eight years to learn," was the way John put it to himself, and his heart sank more and more. Suddenly, he felt an agonizing desire to be able to turn to his father and mother. "I'd give a hundred dollars if I could just go to Father and let him lick me for this," he whispered to the fire. "But," thoughtfully, "I don't believe he would lick me if he knew why I did it. And," he smacked his fist with his palm, "I'm going to get us all to the Willamette, somehow . . . I wish I could see my mother."

He was very tired and he began to cry softly, his head, Francis' fashion, in the crook of his blanketed arm. How long he cried, he did not know, for the first thing he knew, there was a blinding light in his eyes and he opened them full into the rising sun. He jumped up, shouting the rallying-cry of the caravan. "On to Oregon! On to Oregon!" and jerked on his clothes with frantic haste. It was nipping cold. He felt cheerful as a bird.

"Who fed the baby last night?" he asked a few minutes later, as Catherine came out of the tent.

"Didn't you? You always do!" returned the little girl reproachfully. "Perhaps she didn't wake up."

John took the fretting baby from Catherine. "You build the fire and Francis milk, while I tend to her. . . . Poor little thing, with all the mean brothers and sisters starving her to death!"

Henrietta stopped her fretting for a moment at the sound of his voice and attempted a little smile. John kissed her, then held her adroitly in one arm while he filled her bottle and placed it in the ashes of last night's fire which still were warm. When she had emptied the bottle, he changed her to dry clothing, wrapped her in a blanket, and made Elizabeth sit down by the fire and hold her.

He ate an enormous quantity of Indian Jo's dried venison which Catherine had soaked overnight and then fried, after which he said, cheerfully, as he stripped to his breeches:

"It's old Betsy-cow's turn now," and without a further word he led the poor brute into the water and, swimming beside her, headed her for the shore they had left the night before. They made it without much difficulty.

On the bank, John allowed poor Betsy a few moments in which to pant and graze, then he fastened her to the tongue of the cart and again drove her into the water. The wheels were the light forewheels of a prairie schooner, and though it was a hard job, Madame Betsy, her great eyes fastened on the indifferent oxen stuffing themselves with island grass, her huge ears flopping to the cries of the children, whose voices she had known ever since her calf days on the Missouri farm—"Co', boss! Co', boss! Co', Betsy! Co', Betsy!"—made her way slowly but surely after John's dripping blond head, always moving just before her.

Even Francis gave unstinted praise. He was waiting with a towel—a very black towel, of course—with which he rubbed John down.

"Gosh, you are a wonder, old John! I take my hat off to you! I make you a thousand bows! I'll take all your orders for the rest of the day! Here's your pants. Here's your shirt. Cath, hand him that cup of hot soup. While you drink that, John, I shall go kiss the cow. I'd rather kiss her than you, anyhow."

"Go on, you old Pie Biter!" shivered John, grinning sheepishly.

"Let me give John his soup," pleaded Louisa.

"No, I want to! Lemme, please," shrieked Matilda.

"Very p-p-p-popular, I am." John's teeth chattered as he took the cup from Catherine and gulped its contents.

"We won't have to worry about getting to the other shore," said Francis. "Water's not over two feet deep. I tried it."

"Whew! That's a relief! We've got a sweet job to get that cart put together again. Let's work as fast as we can. I want to overtake Uncle Billy soon now," said John.

"Do you think we can?" asked Francis eagerly.

"We've got to!" replied John grimly.

By noon they were safely across the river and following the trail westward along the north bank. They made only about three miles that afternoon. The trail led up and down steep rocky grades, and John made the children walk to ease the team. They were all calculating eagerly now on how soon it would be possible to overtake Uncle Billy, and even little Matilda, whose tiny moccasined feet were ill suited to trotting over the ghastly road, made no complaint because she knew they were hurrying to find her dear Aunt Sally.

It snowed that night, and John was worried in the morning when he saw how completely the trail was blotted out. They broke camp, however, and followed along the river-edge, knowing that they could not be lost, so long as they kept the Snake in sight.

# CHAPTER VIII

## Pop-eyed Charley

A WARM wind rose during the morning, and by mid-afternoon the wagon-ruts were again to be seen, winding among the sagebrush. They led, almost as soon as discovered, to the edge of a canyon and down a difficult trail to the river, which rushed below at a depth of many hundreds of feet. It looked gloomy and dark down there, but at least it was sheltered from the winds, which had grown cold. There might be no grazing for the cattle, but they had been gorged on the island and could stand a little bit of starving.

John thrust a stout cedar pole through the spokes of the wheels to lock them and led the oxen down the steep incline. He carried the baby on one arm as usual. Francis followed behind the cart, leading old Betsy. Catherine followed with the little girls. Zigzag, zigzag, down, down, the cart thrusting hard at the oxen's heels, John's red shirt flapping frightfully near the edge of the trail as it twisted down the canyon wall. Mists of purplish gray swirling over the black waters below hid the banks until they were nearly down, but they could hear, as they descended, the noise of a waterfall.

At the foot of the wall, the trail turned into a clump of willow-trees. Here, with a gasp, John halted the oxen. There were three Indian lodges between the willows and the water's edge, three cone-shaped tents of patched buffalo-hides. A small Indian boy in a twist of blanket spied the Sagers first and shrieked an announcement of their presence in a shrill voice that rose above the falling water. And from the tents came more children and several squaws in rags of indescribable material and filth. Up from the shore came half a dozen

Indian braves, dirty, ragged, with black hair matted about their ugly brown faces.

"All you children stay behind the cart!" ordered John in a voice that *would* quaver a little. "Francis, you get out the guns and give me mine." Then he grinned at the biggest of the braves, who was carrying a huge salmon by the gills. He took off his hat and took two fish-hooks from their carrying-place in the band, pointed to the fish and proffered the hooks.

The Indian grunted, ignoring the fish-hooks and pointing to the gun Francis was standing against the willow-trunk, but John shook his head vigorously. The squaws began to chatter violently and made gestures toward the baby. John nodded and smiled, thrust the hooks back into his hat-band and, turning down the blanket, held up the baby for the Indian women to see. Henrietta was a lovely child, although she was beginning to look very delicate. Even the braves joined in the chorus of comment that greeted her appearance. John thought that Henrietta's sweetness was going to safeguard them all. But this dream did not last long.

The brave who evidently was head of the group waved his hand to attract John's attention, then he tapped three of the Indian children on their heads, after which he tapped his own chest. Obviously he was saying that he was the father of these. Then he pointed, one after the other, to the seven Sagers and waved his hand questioningly.

"You want to know where my father is," said John. "Well, you're not going to be told." He pointed vigorously eastward, closed and opened his eyes and held up one finger.

The brave nodded. It was evident to him that the children's people were one sleep to the east. He turned to the group behind him and spoke at some length. Everyone, even the children, turned east to look up the river.

"You see," said John, for the benefit of Francis, who was standing close behind him with his gun, "if our folks are due along here tomorrow, they may not risk doing any dirty work on us. We'll try to trade with 'em and get out. That old pop-eyed Charley who does the talking is the boss."

Francis' teeth were chattering so he couldn't reply. The poor little girls were huddled against the wagon in a paralysis of fear.

After several minutes of chatter, Pop-eyed Charley, as John had designated him, held up the salmon with one hand and three fingers with the other. It was a very huge price, as John knew from his observations at Fort Hall, but he nodded gravely, gave up the three fish-hooks, and tossed the fish into the cart.

"You girls scuttle back up the trail," he ordered. "Francis, turn the team around and follow."

But at the first attempt of Francis to move the oxen, Pop-eyed Charley sprang forward, struck the boy's hand from the lead-rope, and tried to guide the team toward a clump of grass beyond the willows. The oxen blinked solemnly and, perhaps with ox-like memories of the madness of Dr. Dutch, they did not move. At an order from Pop-eyed Charley, one of the bucks ran lightly up the trail, intercepted the girls and herded them back toward the cart.

John grew pale to the lips. "What do you think you're doing, Old Ugly Face!" he shouted at the buck. "Don't you touch those girls, or I'll shoot you!" He raised his gun.

Ugly Face halted and said something to Pop-eyed Charley. Pop-eyed Charley pointed from the oxen to the grass. Pointed to the fire that burned before one of the tents. Pointed to the cart and from that to a space beyond the third lodge where the ashes of an old fire showed that a fourth had stood.

"He's as good as saying we've got to camp here, Francis. What shall we do?" asked John.

"Do whatever he says, for gosh sake!" quavered Francis. "My hands shake so I couldn't hit the broad side of a canyon."

"Neither could I," muttered John. Then loudly,

"All right, girls! There's nothing to be afraid of.
They want us to camp with them."

He nodded to Pop-eyed Charley and drove the
oxen to the grass-plot, the little girls running to
cover like frightened rabbits under the cart as soon
as it was located. None of the Indians offered to
help the children, but all established themselves
near the cart and watched as though they never
before had seen anything so interesting.

There was more light in the river-bottom than
had appeared from the top. The mists had lifted
and the sunset glow from the sky, so far above, re-
vealed for a short time the details of the children's
prison. There was a wide, grass-grown bank with
willows. There was a little fall, not more than two
feet high, below which the Indians were fishing.
There was the same sort of rocky red wall across
the river as on this side. Below the fall, John thought
there was a ford and that the trail climbed up the
canyon, zigzag, just across the way.

When the tent was set up, in a frightened silence,
the four older children did their usual chores. Elizabeth held the baby. Francis milked the cow. John
started the fire and prepared the baby's bottle.
Catherine cooked the meal. Not until the children
had settled around the fire to eat the salmon Catherine had broiled on little sticks over the coals, did
their chattering audience return to its own business

of cooking and eating. And not until then did John try to discuss their situation with Francis. He sent poor little Catherine limping off to bed with her sisters, built up the fire and told Francis to keep his gun handy.

Then the two boys huddled together before the flames.

"What will they do to us when they find we ain't got any folks coming from the east?" said Francis.

"We've got to get away before that happens," replied John.

"But how can we? Gosh, why did we ever start off by ourselves!" moaned Francis, his little freckled face puckered up to keep the tears back.

"I suppose you'd rather have Henrietta and Matilda taken away from us and we be there at Fort Bridger with old Bridger, getting a licking every five minutes and no chance of starting Father's farm on the Willamette!" exclaimed John.

"Hadn't you rather? Now, honest, John?" asked Francis, wonderingly.

"No, I hadn't," lied John stoutly. "There's nothing to be so scared about. I heard about these Indians in the store at Fort Hall. They're strung all along the Snake and they have a regular fish trade with the Hudson's Bay Company traders. They wouldn't dare to do us harm because they're afraid of the British like they ain't of the Americans, except Kit Carson. I wonder if any of 'em know his name? I'll try it on them tomorrow."

"I'll tell you what," said Francis, his lips quivering, "if we get out of this mess alive, I want to go straight back to Fort Hall."

"We're a lot nearer to Uncle Billy than we are to Fort Hall. Look here, Francis, old boy, have a piece of hoarhound. You'll feel better." John dug a fragment from the depths of his hip pocket.

Francis took the candy. "I know you think I'm a baby," he mumbled.

"I think you're a darned old fool to get worried over the Injuns. They ain't going to hurt us. They're a lot more likely to hide us and send to the Hudson's Bay Company to ransom us. They do that once in a while, I've heard."

"I heard that, too." Francis looked more cheerful. "I don't care much what they do as long as they don't torture us or kill us. Do you think they have any guns?"

"I saw bows and arrows in one of the tents but no guns," replied John.

"But what are we to do, John?" urged Francis.

"Well, you are going to sleep across that tent door with your gun, and I'm going to sit up here with my gun and watch all night. And I'll think of some way out of it. I always do."

"Yes, you always do," echoed Francis sleepily. "Maybe if I'd go now and get a nap I could spell you, if you'd wake me up about midnight."

"Maybe," agreed John. "Go ahead. I'm not afraid."

The Indians tended strictly to their own affairs during the evening. For hours, John sat beside the fire, struggling with his fears, his regrets, and trying to think of some way out of their trouble. After making and rejecting many plans, he hit upon one that he thought would work. He would offer a big fee of tobacco and fish-hooks to Pop-eyed Charley if he would act as their guide to Uncle Billy. The more he turned this idea over in his mind, the more probable it seemed to him that it would work. The relief that came with this thought made it harder than ever to keep awake. He got up and began to pace between the fire and the cart. But he could not keep to that long. John was overworked and underfed and it was impossible for him to keep awake, although he did not know it. He told himself that he was a weak sissy to doze on his feet as he was doing. At last he sank down by the fire, his gun in his lap, and bowed his head on his knees, just, he told himself, for five minutes' rest.

He was not so much exhausted as he had been the night after crossing the Snake, but he was far more tired than any boy of his age ought to be so nature again took control in her own hands and held him locked in dreamless slumber for ten long hours. Rain pattering on his face woke him. He was lying on his back, his feet in the ashes of last night's fire. He crawled stiffly to his feet. It was dull and foggy in the canyon, but still he saw it was daylight. And at once he saw something else. He rubbed his eyes and gasped. The lodges of the Indians were gone! There were no Indians to be seen around the camp.

John ran to the tent and called the sleeping children. They came tumbling out while John, with sudden anxiety, hurried over to the willow grove. No, the cattle were there, contentedly grazing. He rushed back to the tent and looked within it.

"They've robbed us!" he shouted.

Very carefully, the evening before, all the contents of the cart had been packed in the tent. The Indians had taken all their store, the fish-hooks, the tobacco, the pemmican, the dried venison, the precious flour, the ammunition and guns! They had taken the extra blankets, leaving only one apiece. They had not touched the baby's carpet-bag, the cooking utensils or the ax.

The calamity was so terrible that for a long time no one spoke. The baby's wailing finally roused them and, mechanically, John took her from Catherine.

"Build the fire, Catherine," he said dully. "And, Francis, go milk."

"Sure, I will!" gasped Francis. "Gosh! Good riddance to bad rubbish, I say! At least they didn't take our scalps!"

"No, they didn't take our scalps," echoed Catherine. "What shall I cook for breakfast, John?"

"Cook willow leaves!" snapped John. "Why ask me?"

"Because you're always telling us you're boss!" retorted Catherine. "Always telling us you're as smart as a man. Go ahead now, Mr. Smarty, and get us food like a man would."

John glared. "I'm going to give you an old-fashioned whipping, Miss, just as soon as I get this baby fixed up for the day."

"You shan't hit Catherine!" Elizabeth, the seven-year-old, suddenly stamped her foot. "She's all the mother we've got! Louisa and Matilda and I'll bite and scratch you if you touch Catherine. So there now!"

John's hands shook with temper and anxiety. Fortunately, the baby demanded his attention for some minutes and by the time he had put her in order and had fed her, he was calmer and told himself that a family fight would only make matters worse. He gave Henrietta to Elizabeth and walked over to the water's edge to see if there was any hope of finding fish. The Indians had left a rough net of willows and rushes below the dam. John called to Francis to help him lift it, and to their wild delight they brought up three or four fish, weighing altogether about fifteen pounds. They replaced the net and before long a great kettle of salmon was boiling over the fire.

"I think this is a lovely camp," announced Catherine, when everyone had been stuffed to the brim. "It's so much warmer than it is at the top of the canyon. I wish we could stay here a long time and get rested."

"And let the Indians come back and get you?" asked Francis.

"No! I forgot the Indians!" exclaimed Catherine. "I do get so tired of going and going. You folks who aren't lame don't know how hard it is."

"Honest, Catherine, I do get awful sorry about your leg." Francis was rubbing his full stomach contentedly as he spoke.

"I want Uncle Billy. I want him now!" wailed Matilda, who was sitting flat on the ground, her little bruised feet sticking straight in front of her. "I can't walk never no more and Uncle Billy carries me."

John sat silent during this chatter. He was biting his nails and wondering what Kit Carson would

say should be done under these conditions. Suddenly he gave his verdict.

"Now, you young ones listen to me. We can't
move away from this place without a supply of
food. I suppose we could get a lot of fish together,
but it would take a long time to dry it and every
minute Uncle Billy is getting farther and farther
away from us. So I tell you what I'm going to do.
I'm going to butcher one of the oxen. I guess it'll
be old Hiram. He's the oldest and Silas is in better
condition to keep the trail. Then I'm going to take
a three days' supply of meat and leave you folks
here, while I hurry on and overtake Uncle Billy."

A howl of protest rose from every throat but the
baby's. She was whimpering, anyhow, poor mite.
And although this attitude of the children made his
decision that much harder to keep, it warmed John
in his lonely, anxious heart to find that, in spite of
all they said, they really depended on him for safety
and support.

It required the rest of the day to butcher old
Hiram and to hang such portions of him as they
did not cut up for drying, high in the willow-trees.
The task of drying would require several days. John
planned to be back in four, unless by some great
good luck he found Uncle Billy close at hand.

Long before daylight, John had started the fire
and had put the stew-pot on. He was eating his

solitary breakfast when he heard Catherine rousing the other children. Shortly she came out of the tent carrying the Bible.

"It's Sunday, John," she said, plumping the big book down on his knees.

"That's right, I guess it is!" exclaimed John, with a sly glance at Francis.

But Francis only nodded in agreement and stood politely waiting, his tin plate in his hand. John opened to the prayer of Habakkuk. The children listened quietly. The rush of the river, the wail of the wind down the canyon, were the only sounds that rose, except the boyish voice that stumbled in the firelight over the grand old words that Kit Carson loved.

*"The Lord God is my strength and he will make my feet like hind's feet and he will make me to walk upon mine high places—"*

He closed the book gently, kissed the baby, asleep in young Elizabeth's lap, picked up his blanket, in which was rolled a good twenty pounds of boiled beef, and cleared his throat to say fiercely:

"Don't any of you dare to cry or say good-by to me!" and he was off, wading the ford below the falls without once looking back.

All that day and the next John moved rapidly along the trail. He found many traces of Uncle Billy and of other less recent caravans. Fine pieces of furniture, some new-made graves, broken carts, the bones of dead horses. Sometimes the camps were not more than five miles apart, as if they had feared that the next grass and water would be too far away. Sometimes the camps were dry—made far from grass or water—torment for man and beast.

John jogged along wearily but steadily, thankful that three times a day he helped to make lighter the pack on his thin shoulders. It was near sunset of the second day before he caught sight of a human being. It had sleeted all the afternoon and it was not until he saw a fire glowing that he realized that he was nearing a camp. He brought himself up abruptly, in deadly fear of Indians. All about him were tumbled heaps of rocks and no trees. A dreary place for a camp, he thought, wondering of what the fire had been built, as he hid himself behind a rock-heap to spy out the nature of the camp.

He had not to wait long. He heard Adam Polk say, "Some day I'm going to come back from Californy just to lick that Captain Grant."

Adam was not half through the sentence when John started on a staggering run for the camp. There were three tents set in a close triangle with a fire in the center. In the doorway of each tent sat a group of people. John, ragged, dripping, long hair hanging about his face, burst into the scene with a husky cry:

"Where's Uncle Billy Shaw?"

"Great Goshen, it's John Sager!" cried Adam Polk. "Where's the rest of the young ones? Injuns get 'em?"

"Not up to two days ago," panted John. "Where's Uncle Billy?" looking around at the familiar faces of the Polk, Argyle and Lehman families.

"He's hell bent still for the Willamette. We changed our plans and are on the road to Californy. Give the boy some soup, Mary," replied Polk.

But there was no need for this order. All three of the women folks were bustling about. In a moment, John, with a dry shirt on, was sitting in the Polks' tent door, eating a hot supper and telling his adventures.

"We all thought you'd gone back to the States with Kit Carson's outfit," said James Argyle. "How come you to tell that lie?"

John blushed, cleared his throat, then explained. At another time the hearers would have smiled over the boy's explanations, but the situation was too serious. John had complicated the almost insurmountable difficulties of the trail until it was difficult to speak patiently to him.

"Well, what do you expect now?" demanded Adam Polk. "Expect us to take you to Californy with us?"

"I don't want to go to Californy!" exclaimed John huskily.

"You are near twenty miles along the Californy trail now," said James Argyle. "Must have been careless about watching the forks."

"Half the time I couldn't see any trail at all!" cried John. "How far ahead is Captain Shaw?"

"Can't tell. He left us a day back. He was pretty bad with dysentery, and so was Dr. Dutch, so the chance is they've not got very far."

John looked haggardly from one to the other. He didn't want to go to California. More than that, he knew that these people would be almost in despair if he begged them to wait while he brought up the children. They were all haggard with weariness and starvation. Seven more mouths to feed might easily mean starvation and death for many. In common humanity, they would wait; but *John was carrying his father's dream to the Willamette,* and though he had his moments when his will failed him, so far he had not actually taken a backward step.

He cleared his throat. "I want to get to the Willamette," he repeated. "If you folks could sell me a gun and some ball and powder and some blankets and fish-hooks, I can pay for 'em with my father's watch I got around my neck next my skin, where the Injuns didn't get it, you bet. Then I'll go back

and get my family and take 'em along to catch up
with Captain Shaw."

Not a face in the firelight but looked pitifully
relieved.

"We can do better than that," declared Adam
Polk. "We picked up a sick Injun pony on the trail
yesterday. We can't feed him and he's too far gone
for butchering. Would be afraid to eat him, anyhow.
But I guess he would carry you back to your camp.
And you keep your father's watch. Hey, neighbors?"

Everyone nodded approval, Mrs. Polk adding,
"Have you enough clothes for the baby? My little
Myra—" She choked up.

"Drowned in the last crossing of the Snake," said
Adam grimly. "That's what decided us to come this
way. How is the baby?"

"She cries a good deal," replied John, "but I guess
she's all right. I'd be glad for some warm clothes,
Mrs. Polk. You folks are awful kind."

"Everybody better go to bed now," said James
Argyle. "This boy needs all the rest he can get."

# CHAPTER IX

# The Hot Springs

THE pony was as near a mere hide full of bones as a living horse could be, but John managed to make something more than the return trip to the Snake River trail on him, that next day. He made camp near a little meadow of wild hay beside a creek, and the pony ate ravenously half the night. John told himself that there was more of starvation than disease that ailed the little animal. He was mounted long before daylight on the second day of his return trip and by ten o'clock had reached the head of the trail down into the canyon.

He scarcely dared look over the top and sat a full moment staring at the cloudy sky from the pony's back before he found courage to dismount and peer down toward the river. There were mists there, as usual, but he saw the tent and the glow of the fire.

"Hello!" he shouted. "On to Oregon!" and as he plunged down the trail leading the pony, Francis' shrill whistle and Elizabeth's squeals of joy greeted him. Halfway down, Francis appeared with a wide grin.

"Gosh, where'd you steal the horse? Where's Uncle Billy?"

"Everything all right?" cried John. "How's the baby?"

"All well! That baby's the champion yeller of the United States. Where's Uncle Billy?"

John gave a hurried explanation, ending with, "I suppose you and Catherine will be mad because I decided not to go with the Polk outfit."

"Oh, I don't know," returned Francis, with his irrepressible grin. "As long as you feed us as well as you have lately we won't get very mad."

John's welcome from his sisters was enthusiastic enough to have brought a better response from him than his remark, "I'm not going to kiss anybody but the baby. Give her here, Catherine. Did you feed her regular? Gee, she is getting thin!"

"When do we start?" demanded Francis.

"Right now!" replied John.

"Where's Uncle Billy?" cried Catherine.

"You tell her, Francis," said John, "while I put some warmer clothes on the baby. Mrs. Polk's baby got drowned and she gave us its clothes."

With the usual confusion, camp was broken. To Catherine's great grief, John insisted on leaving the cart behind. He knew only too well that with only Silas and the wretched Indian pony they could not hope to drag the cart over the sort of country that lay beyond them. But with Catherine and baby Henrietta on the horse, the other three little girls on Silas, when they were not running along the trail like rabbits, they made astonishing speed for several days. The weather was clear and fine and they gorged on beef, so that they developed more strength than they had felt for several weeks. Only the baby continued weak and ailing. Poor little soul, she could not accommodate herself to the loss of her mother. The cow's milk disagreed with her, and John's ideas of cleanliness were, for all his good intentions, not those of Dr. Dutch.

They all felt so well that the fact that after five days of travel they had not overtaken the Shaws' outfit did not cause them great anxiety. John, indeed, striding along at the head of the cavalcade, the baby on one arm, his gun over his shoulder, began again to tell himself that he could do very well without the grown people. They were growing accustomed now to the loneliness, to the silences broken only by the howl of wolves, by the song of birds if by lucky chance they camped in a cedar-grove, or by the unending rush of waters if they were near the Snake.

All was fine, so long as the good weather lasted. The trail was now working northward with the river, and John was hoping that within a day or so they would reach Fort Boise, the next trading-post belonging to the Hudson's Bay Company, when they woke one morning to a rain and sleet storm of such fury that he dared not take the children out in it. They had made a "dry camp" the previous night, pitching the tent in the shadow of a great black rock that stuck out from a sandhill covered with the usual huge growth of sagebrush. Sandhills lay in every direction, even across the gash of the river, to the east.

They ate a meal of dried beef, for there was no fire-wood, then sat miserably huddled together in the tent. The baby was blue with the cold. John could not endure her whimpering and soon after breakfast he started out to search for fire-wood. The river was deep-buried between sheer black walls down which ran numerous waterfalls and jutting springs, none of which he could reach from the top. Dimly through the sleet he saw, to the west, what looked like a dried creek-bed. Often these creek-beds contained willows and grass near their source. John pulled his ragged black felt hat down firmly, and started at a jog-trot toward the supposed creek. But he did not trot more than a moment. The way was almost impassable with broken black rock-heaps, and these were covered with a curious, white and red crust that reminded John of what he had seen near the famous Bear Springs to the southeast of Fort Hall.

He had not clambered half an hour over the rocks when he observed that, in spite of the sleet and the bitter wind, the air was warmer. Patches of green grass appeared and low-growing willows in leaf. He followed the line of willows, slid over a great black rock and gasped with surprise.

He was standing at the edge of a spring, a spring so hot that it sent a blanket of steam up to meet the driving sleet, a spring so hot that the air all about was that of summer and the sleet was turned to rain. There was an open space perhaps a hundred feet in diameter beyond the spring, bounded by the terrible rock-heaps and set with beautiful willow clumps. Within one of the clumps was an Indian lodge, and as John stood gasping, a man lifted the flap and came out.

Man and boy stared at each other. John saw a half-breed, with a handsome, sullen face, well dressed in deerskin tunic and breeches, with a tarpaulin over his shoulders to shed the rain. He wore a wide hat such as the Spanish trappers round Fort Hall had worn. The half-breed saw a tall boy, thin as a shadow, his ragged red shirt tied up with bits of rope to keep it from dropping altogether from his body, his feet wrapped with strips of oxhide, a boy whose long hair fell over his shoulders and whose blue eyes were startlingly large and clear in his tanned face.

"Hello, stranger!" exclaimed John. "You own this camp?"

"How you say?" demanded the half-breed in a threatening voice.

"I say that I've got five little sisters freezing to death back yonder and I want to bring them up here to get warm, if you won't shoot on sight. My father and mother are dead and we're traveling alone." John drew a little nearer to the warmth of the spring and eyed the stranger closely.

As they stood, glowering at each other, a woman's voice called weakly from the lodge. The man replied, then beckoned to John.

"She say to come in," he growled.

John followed him into the lodge. It was roomy.

There was a heap of skins on either side. Buffalo-hides formed the carpet. A young woman lay on one of the piles of skins, under a red blanket. She was a white woman, with a dark complexion and masses of black curly hair twisted about her head.

"A white boy!" she exclaimed in a low voice, as John came in. "Where are your people?"

John made his explanations while he stared with all his might.

"Of course! Bring them at once!" she said as John finished his statement. "No! No, Juan! This has to be! Go back with the boy and help him."

"I don't want him to go back with me." John jerked his chin defiantly. "He'd do us dirt, being that he don't want us here. And I wouldn't stop, either, you bet, if the baby wasn't so cold."

The young woman shrugged her shoulders. "Very well, boy, do as you wish."

John needed no urging. He made his way back to the tent as fast as he could, what with sleet and broken rock. A little over an hour later he led Silas, with his precious burden, down into the hot springs camping-place. Neither the half-breed nor the young woman appeared while John and Francis were setting up the tent. But when at last that was done, Juan came out from the lodge with a great armload of dry wood which he dropped before the tent.

"She says—bring baby for her e-see," he mumbled, and turned away.

"As soon as I get her fixed up a little!" called John, adding under his breath, "Old Sour Face! Hope he chokes to death!" Then he gave his orders. "Francis, I'll make the fire close up to the entrance, and you cut some willows. It'll burn with all this dry wood to mix with it. Then, Catherine, you and the girls take off your clothes, a piece at a time, and dry them. See?"

"Isn't this a lovely camp!" exclaimed Catherine. "Oh, I'm getting warm already without a fire! Who is the lady, John? Have they seen Aunt Sally and Uncle Billy?"

"Don't jabber so much," replied John, "but get Matilda dried off before she catches lung fever."

The fire blazed up. John washed the baby's delicate little face, gave her some warm milk, then carried her over to the lodge. Juan was sitting sulkily on one of the beds of skins. The young woman lay, as before, on the other. She sat suddenly erect, however, as John came in.

"Put her down here beside me, boy!"

Obediently, John cast aside the blanket, damp with rain, and laid the baby, wrapped in a fold of buffalo-pelt, upon the young woman's bed. She stared at Henrietta for a long moment; then, shaking her head, she said, as if to herself:

"So far away! So far away! What is the good God

thinking of? Or has the Blessed Virgin forgotten women? How beautiful, but how delicate! Boy," looking at John, "she cannot live without a woman's care."

John's heart gave a great thud and he bent anxiously over Henrietta, who lay with her blue eyes fastened on the lodge roof. "She don't look much thinner than she was when we left Fort Hall. And if Aunt Sally had her, she couldn't feed her nothing different than we do."

The young woman clasped her slender hands together and rocked herself back and forth.

"What a land! What a terrible land! Where even the little babies starve!"

"Are you sick or hungry, ma'am?" asked John. "Because we've got about a ton of dried beef with us. We've been drying some every night for I don't know how long. And you're welcome to some."

"We're hungry," replied the young woman, "weak from hunger. We have been robbed by Indians of everything except what is in this lodge. Juan, go and see if the children really have some to spare. I'll care for the baby, boy."

For the first time, the sullenness lifted from the half-breed's face.

"Come on, Yawn," grinned John, "though you don't look so much like a yawn to me as you do like a sure-enough bite!"

Juan actually smiled as he followed John out into

the warm rain. "You look lak bear bite, you, eef hongry lak me!" he said.

John gave him a curious glance and said, "You wait here while I go in the tent."

The girls were playing Indians, wrapped in blankets while their clothing dried. Francis was trying to oil and clean the gun.

"What's loose, John?" he asked.

"These folks are hungry," replied John.

"For gosh sake, give them a lot of that beef, then," grinned Francis. "Pretty soon you'll have to be saying 'gee-haw' to me, for I'll have turned into old Hiram's ghost."

"Ain't going to risk starving our own crowd, I can tell you that, old trapper," replied John, emerging from the tent, however, with at least twenty-five pounds of dried beef.

The half-breed filled his mouth ravenously, as he seized the pile and turned back to the lodge.

The young woman was holding the baby when the two came in. "O Blessed Virgin, at last you did give ear to me!" she cried as she saw the strips of beef. "Start a fire, Juan, and stew it. Starved as I am, I cannot endure the smell uncooked. Boy, sit here and tell me how we can repay you."

John grinned and shook his head. "Pass it on to the next one you find hungry, I guess. Which way are you folks going?"

The Señorita shook her head and her eyes filled

with tears. "Before we were robbed, we were going to Fort Uncompahgre in the Spanish Rockies, which is owned by my friend, Don Luis."

She paused, her eyes on the fire Juan was kindling at the door. John's mind was in confusion. He was certain that this was the young woman whom Kit Carson was seeking and he thought that perhaps in her distress she might be glad to know of Kit. Yet he dared say nothing. And the scout, undoubtedly, was working toward the Spanish fort which John knew lay far to the southeast of Fort Hall.

"Did you come from California?" he asked finally.

"Yes, poor fool that I am!" exclaimed the Señorita. "I thought that Juan there, being half Indian, would have me safe at Fort Uncompahgre by September. It seems, however, that he is—" Again she paused.

John wriggled. His curiosity was very great. "He's your half-brother, isn't he?"

The Señorita gave him an indignant look. "That is not a polite remark, boy. My mother was an English lady."

"Oh, that's why you talk English, then!" John nodded. "I didn't mean to be impolite, Miss. I'd like to help you, honest. Why don't you come along up to Fort Boise with me? You could get a new outfit there, maybe."

The Señorita gave a startled gasp. "We are near Fort Boise? No! No! I cannot go to an English fort. My father is being friends with the English."

"I should think that would be a good reason for going, then," suggested John.

She shook her black head. "You don't understand." She looked at him for a long moment, then added, "I must trust you. You are faithful to this baby. I believe that you will be faithful to me. You are white and nearly a man. My father was making me marry an Englishman. I am running away to marry Don Luis Velasquez. He is very poor, but he will make himself rich with furs."

"Why didn't you tell your father you wouldn't?" asked John. "That's what an American girl would do."

The Señorita's eyes widened. "But not at my age? I am sixteen only."

"Only three years older than me!" murmured John. "Golly!"

Juan came in with a steaming pan and John picked up the baby. "Guess I'll go get some dinner, myself," he said.

"Then you'll come back and help me?" asked the Señorita.

"I'll come back," replied John. "But I'm not sure I can spare you more grub."

"That's not it!" exclaimed the girl.

"I can't promise blind," said John, none the less firmly because he grinned.

Then Henrietta began to cry and he hurried out.

# CHAPTER X

# The Camp in the Larches

THE rain ceased at noon and the sun came out brightly. The younger Sager children were enchanted with the new camp. Its warmth, the enclosing ring of rocks which made such a secret spot of it, the wonderful spring which boiled so strangely, the flowers that bloomed in the grass! Even Francis joined in teasing John to stay for a long, long rest in "this lovely camp." They were finishing their dinner when John put an end to their pleas.

"I get so tired of moving," said Catherine, her

lower lip quivering, as she pushed her wild chestnut hair back from her thin little cheeks, which had lost all their pretty color. "Seems as though I'd been limping and moving and moving and limping for a hundred years."

"Don't you want to do what Father wanted?" demanded John.

"Seems as though he'd been dead five hundred years," was Catherine's response, with a little sob. "How do we know what he'd want?"

Indeed, the sufferings on the trail were dimming the younger children's grief at the loss of their father and mother. John could not understand that this was a natural thing. He stared at Catherine as though she had uttered an oath.

"How do we know what he'd want?" he shouted. "You bad, disobedient girl! You didn't love your father, that's sure. He wanted us to go to the Willamette in Oregon, and you know it as well as I do! And that's where we're going! 'Rest in this lovely camp,'" he ended, with a squeaking imitation of Catherine, and strode away toward the Señorita's lodge.

He was still red with anger when he entered; but the young Spanish girl was too much filled with her own troubles to inquire about John's. She was sitting on the side of her bed talking to Juan. John thought that, if she were not so dark, she would have been very pretty. No woman not as fair as his mother could be really lovely in John's eyes. She wore a dark, close-fitting riding-suit which was utterly unsuited to the trail. Indeed, she seemed to have discovered that, for she had cut the long skirt off, halfway to her knees.

"I feel so much stronger, boy!" she exclaimed. "You have been our kind savior. And now look! I have plenty of money. You are going up to Fort Boise and buy us a new outfit and bring it back to us, while we look out for your brother and sisters. And there will be enough money for you to buy yourself a horse."

"Why don't you send Yawn?" asked John. "I can show him the way."

"But Juan must not be seen. My father will have Juan killed if he is seen. That is why we got lost. We dared not go on the trails."

"I don't see why you want to get married, anyhow!" exclaimed John. "Gosh! You are only three years older than me and I'd rather be fried in hot tallow than get married."

"But I don't want to get married!" cried the Spanish girl. "You are very stupid. That's why I ran away!"

"But you say you are going to marry that fellow at the Spanish fort," insisted John.

She tossed her hands impatiently. "What else can

I do to get from my father's clutches? Don Luis is
a good man, my cousin. I have known him always.
I don't like him much, but I do not hate him, which
I do the Englishman."

All this was rather disgusting to John and if it had
not been for the thought of Kit Carson, he would
have been tempted strongly to tell her that she was
as silly as Catherine. And with the thought of Kit
Carson came the recollection that if the friendship
of this silly girl's father could be won, it might help
win California for America. Of course, he told himself, California was not as important to him as was
Oregon, but it was all for America, so he was bound
to do what he could—that is, anything that would
not interfere with his carrying out his father's
desires.

"I can't go up to Fort Boise and come back,
Miss," he said. "It's awful late in the season for
immigrants and every day we delay makes my children suffer more with the cold. And I'm trying to
overtake those people I told you about. They're all
the folks we got. You let Yawn come with me to
within a mile of Fort Boise. I'll buy the horses and
grub and take 'em back to him. See?"

"And leave me here alone!" cried the Señorita.
"I dare not! Nor must Juan be seen on the trail, even
with you."

John scratched his head, thoughtfully.

"Come, boy, I'll give you money for two horses!" cried the Spanish girl.

"But that don't stop the snows in the mountains and the freezing sleet-storms for these children of mine!" cried John, impatiently. "Don't be so selfish! There's other troubles in the world besides yours. Give me time to think!"

Instead of answering angrily, the Señorita suddenly smiled. Juan spoke for the first time. He seemed a stupid sort to John.

"We both go-a elong off the trail to Fort Boise, Señorita. Sabe?"

"That's a fool notion," said John. "You haven't any outfit." Then he added wistfully, "I wish you could travel with us. It's awful lonesome, just young ones with me."

"I do not dare," repeated the Señorita. "If it were an American fort, all would be well. I like Americans."

"Do you know any American men besides me?" asked John.

"Yes. I know Lieutenant Frémont and Sir Christopher Carson!" Suddenly she clasped her hands. "Him, I would love to marry!"

"Oh, for heaven's sake!" roared John. "Can't you think about anything but marrying? This is serious!" Then, as the Spanish girl gave him a haughty look, he added, "Kit Carson's a good friend of mine. Saw

him a couple of weeks back, at Fort Hall." He
watched the Señorita closely as he gave this in-
formation.

"If I could find him," she said, "I would be safe.
He would help me, if you will not."

"I'm doing the best I can," replied John. "You
better get your nerve up and come with me. Somehow we'll make out. I always do. There ain't anybody on the trail now but Injuns. Come now, Miss.
You eat a lot the rest of the day, and tomorrow,
before dawn, we'll start."

"Señorita"—suddenly Juan, who had stuffed himself until he was sleepy, opened his eyes—"it's the
only way!"

The Spanish girl groaned and threw herself back
on the bed of skins. "Go away, boy, and I will
think," she commanded; and very gladly John de-
parted.

It was after sunset, and all the children, dried
and warm and full of beef, had gone to bed, save
John, who sat by the fire holding Henrietta and trying to hush her feeble crying, when Juan came up
and squatted beside him.

"She ees afraid to go weeth you-a," he said. "She
ees afraid to stay-a. I theenk we both stay-a. We
buy more meat from you-a. You-a send Injun back
with horse and meat. I keep-a Injun so he no go and
tell. Sabe?"

John weighed the idea carefully. He needed money very badly. All that his parents had left had gone to Captain Bridger. He could spare a hundred pounds of beef and still have several days' supply left. Also, it was necessary, if he was to help Kit Carson, to keep the Señorita from starving to death. John, finally and reluctantly, for the responsibility of feeding so many people weighed heavily on him, agreed to Juan's proposal. He told himself, as Juan left him, that, somehow, he would send word to the scout of the Señorita's whereabouts.

The morning dawned clear and fine. The Señorita —selfishly, as John thought, and he was right—did not appear to see the little cavalcade start, but Juan was out early. He seemed a very simple fellow and showed a childish liking for John. He helped to make up the packs—there was very little to pack since Pop-eyed Charley's departure—and helped the children to establish themselves among the blanket-rolls on the broad back of Silas. It was terribly dangerous riding for such young children. Juan, having lifted Matilda to Elizabeth's lap, shook his head and ordered everyone to halt. Then he ran into the lodge.

He returned carrying two new willow pack-baskets which he told John he had woven at the springs to replace those that had been stolen. He could make another pair easily. In the meantime,

these were "plenty large" to act as carrying-baskets
for Matilda and Louisa. To the children's interest
and delight he slung the baskets by ropes across
Silas' back, "lak een Spaneesh countree," so that
they balanced each other against the beast's ribs. He
lifted Louisa into one and Matilda into the other.

"Gosh!" cried Francis. "They're as safe as papooses in their cradles!" Then he uttered the rallying-cry of the trail. "Catch up! Catch up, you slug-
gards! On to Oregon!"

And so the trail once more.

To the awful beauty of the country into which
they now were moving, the children were indifferent. It offered them only weariness and suffering in
exchange for any admiration they might feel, and
so they stared at the beautiful distant peaks, at the
great white frothing waterfalls that burst from the
black canyon walls and rushed in a thousand rain-
bow colors into the green water of the Snake, only
with dislike and fear.

The third day after leaving the hot springs, in
the afternoon, as they were moving slowly over a
country that seemed to be made up of little red
rocky hills, running one into the other, two Indians
appeared from the north. They were leading a
small string of pack-ponies. John, his heart in his
throat, drew his little company up at the side of the
trail and prayed, very earnestly, that the Indians
would pass in a hurry.

Of course, he was praying against the very nature of things, and so there was no answer to his prayer. The Indians drew up and sat silently staring. They both were a little better covered than Pop-eyed Charley's gang had been. The older Indian, very old, wore a blanket coat that still held together despite its rents and rags, and the younger Indian was dressed in an old blue cape and deerskin breeches. Both were unspeakably filthy and ragged, yet, compared with the average Snake River Indian, they were magnificent.

Francis, leading old Betsy, drew closer to John. "Ask the papa how far to Fort Boise. He looks almost kind. The son don't."

John jerked his thumb northward. "Fort Boise?" Then he closed his eyes, opened them, and held up two fingers. "How many sleeps? Two?"

"Five sleep," replied Papa. "Heap slow for you. We make 'em two sleep."

Delighted to find that the old man could speak English, John asked at once, "Did you see any white people up ahead? They're our people. We're trying to catch up with them."

The Indian shook his head. "We come short way whites no sabe."

"You Hudson's Bay Company Injuns?"

"No! Me Cayuse. Live at Dr. Whitman's place. Where you going?"

"To the Willamette," replied John, beginning to

feel very sure that there would be no trouble with these Red Men. "Where's a good place to camp tonight?"

The younger Indian spoke for the first time. "Across river, one mile," pointing back over the way he had come.

"Is it good crossing?" John's heart sank. The animals had forded the Snake five times in three days. Twice he had taken the girls over on rafts made of willows and rush bundles covered with buffalo-pelts.

"Heap bad!" replied the younger Indian. "How much you give if we put you over?"

"I will give you ten fish-hooks," answered John.

"Fifteen!" exclaimed Papa suddenly.

"All right," John sighed. "It's all I got. How many more times have I got to cross this dirty stream before I get to the Blue Mountains?"

"You cross 'em here. You cross 'em after Fort Boise. No more," replied Papa.

"Half the fish-hooks now. Half after cross!" suggested the younger Indian.

"All right, Sonny!" John took the precious packet from the blanket-roll behind Catherine on the pony. He was feeling cheerful at the thought of help at even this far-too-high price. "Seven now. Eight later. And. say, I know how you can earn real money."

"How?" grunted Sonny.

"I won't tell you till you get us safe into a good camp for the night," retorted John.

The two Indians grinned.

"Heap smart boy!" grunted Papa. "Come!"

The Indians turned their little string of six ponies, and John, carrying the gun and leading Silas, followed. Next came Catherine and Henrietta on the drooping horse, whom the children had named Thunder after Kit Carson's big black stallion. Francis brought up the rear with Betsy.

It did not seem so frightening as usual to descend into the canyon and stand beside the sweep of waters, which were about a quarter of a mile wide here. Even the "twins" forgot to scream with fear of Indians, for they were happy to be ferried by people who they had learned, far back on the Platte, understood the crossing of rivers. This was to be even simpler than Indians usually made the ferrying. Papa grunted at Sonny and Sonny, sliding from his pony, disappeared behind a great heap of rocks. He reappeared in about fifteen minutes, paddling along the shore in a log dugout big enough to hold all the girls beside the paddler. In less than an hour the crossing was completed without a tear, even from Matilda.

Standing beside the dripping animals, John paid over his eight fish-hooks.

"Now where's that camping-place?" he asked.

"We'll show," replied Sonny, mounting his shivering mare.

He led the way up the canyon wall, around tumbled rock-heaps, followed the top for a short distance, then, through a break in what had appeared to be solid rock, he led them out into a grove of mighty larch-trees, through which rushed a little brook. The last red light of the sun filtered through the trees as Sonny pulled up his panting horse.

"Now! You tell 'em how make money!" he grunted.

"Sure I will!" cried John, his heart full of gratitude to the first Indians he had met who had kept faith with him. "Are you going to camp here for the night? Where are you headed for, anyhow?"

"We go down Bear River to big Salt country where keep warm all winter," replied Papa. "Heap cold up Dr. Whitman."

"Then you're in no hurry. Have some beef-stew with us and we'll talk," suggested John.

"Good!" grunted Papa, dismounting and preparing to stake his pony out for the night.

"They act like good men," whispered Catherine to John as she helped him unpack the beef. "O John, let's stay a day or so in this lovely camp! I'm so tired and little Matilda is half sick."

"Don't begin that!" shouted John.

"You don't have to yell at me," whimpered Catherine. "At least, you can ask them to guide us for a while. Maybe Dr. Whitman has made them into Christians."

"Can't," replied John. "Gotta keep my word to Yawn and the Spanish girl. And there's more than that to it."

"What more?"

"Aw, things a girl couldn't understand in a thousand years!" John undid the last rope around the pack with the contemptuous sniff that always upset his oldest sister.

"Smarty! You think you're so smart!" She put her tongue out. John promptly boxed her ears and strode away to help Francis put up the tent.

It was very cold. The edges of the little brook were freezing, but with an enormous fire before the tent, the children did not care. At the moment supper was finished and the children sat with the two Indians before the blaze, John felt but one anxiety. Little Henrietta, lying in his lap, refused her bottle! She only turned her head feebly away with the little smile she had for John. He looked at Papa, who sat beside him.

"Do you know why she won't eat?" he asked.

"Cow's milk poison!" The Indian spat with a violent grimace of disgust. "Mother's milk for babies.

You find squaw with papoose, pay her feed your baby."

It was John's turn to feel violent aversion, but he did not express it and he scowled fiercely at Francis and Catherine, who were grinning at each other and pretending to feel sick. The squaws, as they knew them, were filthy beyond words.

"How we get that heap money?" asked Sonny, who was warming buffalo-tallow in the fire and rubbing it into his hair, while the "twins" and Matilda watched him with open mouths, undoubtedly resolving to add this performance to their game of Indians.

John rubbed the baby's hands gently while the Indians eyed him curiously. This white boy must have interested them, strangely, with the queer mixture of bullying and tenderness with which he governed his little tribe. Certainly, no Indian lad would lower himself by taking care of a papoose, a girl papoose at that, as this blue-eyed white boy was taking care of the sickly little object in the blanket.

"Well," said John, "do you know about some hot springs, two miles west of the trail, about three sleeps back from here?"

Sonny shook his head and looked at his father. The old Indian scratched his dirty chin and mumbled to himself for a moment, then nodded. "I sabe.

Some years dries up. Some years good. Last time there, ten years back, all dried up. Injuns no go there now."

"Well, it's going hard now, and must have been a few years, because the willows are big enough to burn. I found it, looking for wood. And in a lodge there I found a white girl and a half-breed. They had a lodge and bedding and nothing else. Indians had robbed them of their whole outfit. Now they want to get to Fort Um—"

John paused, troubled. He could not recall the difficult name. He shook his head. "A Spanish fort, way down in the Rocky Mountains, southeast of Fort Hall. You sabe?"

The two Indians talked to each other at length, but evidently couldn't solve the riddle, for Sonny said at last, "No sabe."

"It doesn't matter, anyhow," John went on, "because I've got a different idea. They wanted me to go to Fort Boise and get an Injun to take some ponies and food down there to them, and they'd pay gold for it and keep the Injun and pay gold for him to guide them to this fort. Seems the girl doesn't want anyone to see her, so they have to keep off the regular Oregon Trail."

"Couldn't guide to fort never heard of," mumbled Papa.

"No, you couldn't," agreed John; then he paused.

"Catherine, you take Matilda to bed before she goes to sleep in the fire. Elizabeth and Louisa, you tumble along, too."

"Aren't sleepy. Aren't goin' to bed," declared Matilda, opening her big blue eyes very wide.

"Neither am I," echoed Louisa, sturdily, pushing her wonderful mass of curls over her little shoulder, which showed bare through the rags of her woolen dress.

"Francis, take Henrietta!" ordered John. "We'll see who's boss in this camp!"

But before he could rise, the three littlest girls had flown into the tent and Catherine had gone limping after them.

Sonny grinned. "Heap big chief boss little squaws!"

John flushed uncomfortably. "Can't help it," he said. "They're awful wild. Well, to get on with my idea. Do you sabe Kit Carson?"

Both Indians nodded energetically.

"Do you trust his word?" continued John.

"Yes. Good Injun like him. Bad Injun run," replied Papa.

"They sure do," agreed John. "Now, Kit Carson, he's my friend and all us children's friend." He paused to tell the story of Carson's introduction to the Sager family and of the Indian fight. The two Indians listened with intense interest, grunting and breathing heavily while John, assisted by Francis, described the scout's activities on that not-to-be-forgotten day and night.

"So you see, we sabe him good," ended John.

Sonny and Papa nodded violently.

"All right!" sighed John, who was weary of talking. "Now, at Fort Hall, Kit Carson told me he was looking for a Spanish girl and her half-breed brother who had run away up into this country from California. What I want you to do is to go down to the hot springs, sell them part of your outfit and get real gold for it. They'll think they are keeping you prisoners to guide them to Fort Um—well, this Spanish fort none of us sabe. You say, all right. Then you guide them to Kit Carson, tell him about me, and he'll give you more gold. And I think the girl will, too. She told me she liked him. But don't you tell them a word about Carson. Or anyone else about him."

"You make paper talk to girl. You make paper talk to Kit Carson," ordered Papa, with the grunt of satisfaction peculiar to an Indian.

"I haven't any paper!" John spoke dejectedly.

"I fix 'em!" exclaimed Sonny. He disappeared into the darkness. When he came back he was carrying two pieces of pale yellow bark about six inches square. John gave the baby to Francis, who promptly carried her into the tent and laid her beside the sleeping Catherine, then hurried back to the fire. John was scratching his messages on the bark with the point of his hunting-knife. They were very short.

Spanish girl and Yawn pay these Injuns good. John Sager.

Kit Carson pay these Injuns if they bring you the Spanish girl all rite. John Sager.

He read the messages aloud.

Sonny grunted, rolled the bark, tied it with a bit of deer-sinew, and grinned broadly at John. "Heap smart boy!"

Papa rose. "Heap good boy! You come by Whitman mission next spring we show you. Good-by."

"How come, good-by?" demanded John.

"We start now. No let other Injun find Spanish girl!" Papa held out a dirty hand to John and shook hands with him and with Francis. The grinning Sonny followed, and then the two stalked off to their horses. In an astonishingly short time, the two boys heard the rapid thud of hoofs that grew less and less until the sighing silence of the larches was all that remained.

"I wish they were going to guide us instead of that selfish Spanish hussy," yawned Francis.

"So do I," agreed John, rolling himself in his blanket.

# CHAPTER XI

# Fort Boise

THEIR camp the next night, after five miles over broken stone, was made without water or grass. Matilda was sick. The older children thought perhaps she was bilious. But the little thing really was sick from weariness. She was so utterly tired that she had become feverish. All day they had met no living soul nor had they found a trace of immigrants along the trail, which was faint at first and often lost for hours in a maze of greasewood.

They had, of course, no stored-up strength to call on, when their days were hard, so they made camp in poor fashion that night. John and Francis could scarcely erect the tent, after the terrible tramping. And Catherine sobbed with weariness into the soup-kettle that barely steamed over the wretched grease-wood fire. It was bitter cold, and coyotes howled, as they will on frosty nights when the stars are bright. There was no hope of building a fire that would keep alive all night. So John crept into the tent for warmth.

Sleet wakened him, long after day had dawned. He roused the children and made his stiffened way out to help Francis kindle a fire. They were grubbing out greasewood roots with their hunting-knives, when a cry from Catherine brought them back to the tent. She was holding up the blanket in which the beef was carried. It was mauled and torn.

"The coyotes have got every speck of beef!" she wailed. "You boys forgot to bring it into the tent last night."

John and Francis looked at each other. But the situation was too bad to be helped by calling names.

"We'll have to get a jack-rabbit or an antelope for sure today," said John with unusual meekness. "Hold out the baby's share of the milk and give the rest to the 'twins' and Matilda for breakfast."

"You know there ain't two cups of old Betsy's

milk left after baby has her share!" scolded Catherine.

"Well, we didn't mean to do it!" shouted Francis.
"Gosh! You are crosser than an old woman!"

"Come, Francis," said John, "we'll pack up and
get going. We must be within a few hours of Fort
Boise."

But he was whistling to keep up his courage and
that of the others.

Two days later there crept up to the gates of
the little stockade that surrounded the cabin that
made up the trading-post known as Fort Boise, a
boy, bearing a baby in his arms. Except for ragged
buckskin breeches and still more ragged moccasins,
the boy was naked. His sun-faded blond hair fell to
his shoulders in tangled profusion. His eyes were
startlingly blue in a face that seemed to be one enormous freckle. He was terribly thin.

The gates were wide ·open and the factor in
charge, a Scotchman named McKay, was standing
before his house door smoking. As he jerked his
pipe from his mouth, the better to express his astonishment, a smaller boy staggered up, leading a pack-
train, and from the strange assortment of animals
there at once disembarked such a rabble of wild,
half-naked little girls as the Scotchman never had
seen even among Indians.

"What is all this!" gasped McKay.

"We're the Sager children," replied John, huskily.
"We haven't eaten for two days. Lost our beef. Lost
our trail."

"Henri!" shouted McKay. "Bring bread and a pail
of milk, with all the tin cups in the house. You children pack yourselves round this table," leading the
way into the one large room in the house.

A half-breed appeared as the children obeyed;
and as the younger children gobbled and tore at
the bread, the Scotchman turned to John, who had
tossed off a cup of milk and now stood gnawing at a
chunk of bread with some semblance of self-control.

"How about the baby?" asked the factor.

"She won't eat," replied John. "I've got to do
something. Is there a white woman around here?"

"Not any. Eat your grub, lad, then give me the
story. Henri, put on a big kettle of stew. What's
the matter with that littlest girl?", pointing to Matilda. "Why don't she eat?"

"She's sick," volunteered Catherine, who had
eaten all she could hold. "Says she's too tired to
eat."

"Wouldn't be surprised if that's right. I've been
so myself," said McKay. He lifted Matilda from the
bench and, holding her in his lap, said with sur-
prising gentleness, "Here, sister, drink one cup of

this nice milk and I'll let you go to sleep in my bed over there."

Matilda looked up at him with heavy eyes and, sip by sip, under the factor's urging, took down the milk. This done, the Scotchman, awkwardly, as if he were not used to handling children, carried her to his bunk. Almost at once she fell asleep. In the meantime the other children had finished eating. The "twins" had laid themselves on the flat floor, drowsily content. Catherine sat with her lame leg stretched out on the bench, her head nodding on her shoulder. Francis established himself in a buffalo-hide chair, a grin of satisfaction on his wizened little face.

"Now, lad," said the Scotchman, "let's have the story."

"We're the Sagers," mumbled John wearily. "John, Francis, Catherine, Elizabeth, Louisa, Matilda, Henrietta Naomi. We were with General Gillian's Oregon Colony, with Captain Shaw. Father and Mother died. Captain Shaw wanted to break up the family. And so—"

"How do you mean, break up the family?" interrupted the factor. "Don't tell me more than you have to, John, my lad, just to show me what's to be done."

John nodded and, with considerable help from McKay, managed to get into words the main facts of the story. When he had finished, he said, "I'll try to get baby to take some warm milk; then, if you'll let me, I'll sleep awhile before I tell you more."

He induced Henrietta to swallow two or three spoonfuls of milk, then he laid her beside Matilda, dropped to the floor and slept. Two hours later the factor shook him.

"Come, John, my lad! Come! You must eat again!"

John sat up stiffly. "Where's the baby?" he asked.

"On the bed, safe enough. Come over to the table, John," this with a kindly hand under John's arm.

"Where are the other children?" demanded John, looking about the room, which was flooded with sunset light, but empty of children save for Matilda asleep again beside the baby.

"Oh, they're outside looking round! Henri stuffed them again with venison-stew and more milk and they're fine. The three-year-old ate well, too."

John silently disposed of a great plate of stew and felt his strength and courage returning like a miracle. The mist that had bewildered him for a day cleared from his brain. He looked at McKay as if he never before had seen him. A big man, with a red beard and hard gray eyes.

"I'll pay you for all you do for me," said John.

"Havers, lad!" exclaimed McKay in a big bass voice. "I'm a human being if I am a bachelor! You're welcome to this and a lot more. You told me you are wishing to overtake Captain Shaw. They passed through here a week ago. But yesterday an Indian came back with an order for beef. Seems that dysentery attacked them again, and the rest of the outfit had been obliged to leave Shaw and his wife, with Dr. Dutch, at the Grande Ronde. They are at the Grande Ronde now, but they are in no shape to take care of seven children. Especially that baby. I'd say that the only thing on earth could save that baby would be for it to be lying in Mrs. Whitman's lap this moment. She makes miracles happen with these Indian babies. A squaw has about as much ability as a cow to take care of a child."

John got up from the bench, walked over to the bed and looked at little Henrietta Naomi. She returned his gaze with the glassy stare of a baby who is slowly dying from lack of proper food. When he came back to the bench, the factor noticed that, in spite of the cold night, beads of sweat stood on the boy's lips.

"She *can't* die! My mother left her to me. She's my child. They're all my children." John spoke brokenly, more to himself than to the factor.

McKay sat smoking, his eyes first on John, then on the motionless bundle on the bed.

"How old are you, John?" he asked, finally.

"Thirteen," replied John.

"Humph!" grunted McKay, and cleared his throat. "Well, ye must have been a great comfort to your parents when they were living."

"That's just the point!" ejaculated John. "I wasn't. Now I'm trying to make up for it. And I'm going to keep the family together, and I'm going to get Father's farm going on the Willamette!"

McKay cleared his throat again. "Henri," he said, "more logs on the fire. It's growing cold." A pause, then he said, "That German doctor might help the baby if he was here but—"

"No, he couldn't," interrupted John. "As I see it now, he nor Aunt Sally Shaw, neither, knew how to feed Henrietta. She was ailing and crying all the time when they were taking care of her. Aunt Sally never had any children and Uncle Billy said Dr. Dutch was no better than a cow-doctor. Are the Whitmans kind people?"

"The best in God's world," replied McKay promptly. "I traveled with them for weeks when they were coming into this country in 1836, and I've been at Waii-lat-pu, their mission, often since. Mrs. Whitman is an angel from heaven if ever there was one. She lost her own little girl by drowning, a while back. She'd always done what she could for the Indian babies, but since her own died she's doubled her efforts. I picked up a baby from a dead squaw some twenty miles from the mission, a year ago. I'd say it was as bad off as yours. I took it to Mrs. Whitman and she never gave up, day or night, till she'd got its little works to going again. But I got to be honest with you, lad. I don't think your baby will live till you get there."

"She's got to!" said John through set teeth. "If you'll sell me a quarter of beef and maybe some flour, we'll start tomorrow."

"Leave the little girls here, and come back for them, or I'll try to send them after you," suggested McKay.

John gave the Scotchman a grateful little smile, but shook his head. "I promised my mother we'd stick together. I guess if we've come through this far, we can stand anything that's ahead of us. I'm going to get the baby up to Mrs. Whitman."

The Scotchman looked at the fire. There were many protests he might have made. But a curious feeling had come to McKay while talking to the boy. It was as if John had to go on just as he was going, as if some power greater than that of any of the grown people that the children had met, was urging and leading John westward. After several more pulls at his pipe, the factor said:

"God help you, lad! Your animals are not so bad as might be expected. Guess there are some Indians hanging round outside. I'll find a couple of reliable ones to take you to the Grande Ronde. You can pack

on my horses so that your animals can get well rested
for the crossing of the Blue Mountains. I'd go with
you, myself, only I have to start for Fort Hall tomorrow, where Captain Grant lies at death's door."

"I can pay the Injuns," said John.

"Very well," agreed McKay. "Now you'd better
round up your tribe and all of you go to sleep again.
I'll wake you all in a couple of hours for another
feed."

With the thought of Mrs. Whitman, new hope
had flooded John's heart and he went to bring in
the children with renewed strength and courage.

It was still dark the next morning when McKay
started the little cavalcade off with a broad Scotch
"God be wi' ye!"

He had the name of being a hard man, did Factor McKay. But that this children's crusade sort of
thing was more than he could bear with his usual
cold blood, we have proof in a letter he wrote to his
mother in Scotland:

I suppose my letters to you since I left home have
contained many strange tales. But none that twisted
me like this. They were a scourge to have about one,
I assure you, but nothing could lessen the pathos of
them. That lad John! Surely the Heavenly Father
must have been moved by the lad's vicarious father-
hood. Not, you must understand, that he was any
gentle guardian! He took no nonsense from any of

them. When the girl of eight or nine protested against holding the baby, he handed the baby to his brother, jerked his sister across his knee and clouted her until she begged to nurse young puling Henrietta. The strain had told on him. He was like young mothers I have seen. All nerves and unable to throw off the torture of responsibility. By Jove, he ruled me, too, for I sent them on, after a night's sleep, under the care of a pair of good Indians and fresh horses.

# CHAPTER XII

# The Grande Ronde

IT was on a biting cold afternoon of mid-October that the Indians led the children up the valley of the Grande Ronde in what is now northeastern Oregon, and halted with them before a camp containing two tents and a two-wheeled cart. No one was to be seen about, but at John's shout, a weak voice answered from the larger tent:

"Everybody sick!"

John ordered the other children to keep back. Then he got down from his horse, gave the baby to Catherine, and lifted the tent flap. Three living skeletons lay huddled under blankets on the ground: Aunt Sally, Uncle Billy, Dr. Dutch.

"John Sager!" came at the same time from three feeble throats, Uncle Billy adding, "Where's Kit Carson?"

John grinned. "I never did see him! We've been following you all this time, trying to catch up."

He told the story of his "double cross," the elders listening in angry amazement.

Aunt Sally tried to rise to her elbow, but fell back. "Is the baby there?"

John's grin disappeared. "Yes; she's very bad off."

"You haf murdered her!" Dr. Dutch still had sufficient strength to glare at John.

"I hope you brought grub," Uncle Billy said. "We've only got a little beef. It would see us through the Blue Mountains, but not six more mouths! We're awful sore at you, John Sager."

"Guess maybe we'd better move right on!" John drew himself up stiffly. "I hadn't planned to stay only tonight, anyhow. I'm going to get the baby up to Mrs. Whitman as quick as I can."

Aunt Sally groaned. "If I wasn't so awful sick and weak! Bring her in and let the doctor and me see her."

"No, I ain't going to do that. Seems to me that dysentery is about the only thing she hasn't got," replied John firmly, feeling a vast relief that he had an excuse for not hearing Aunt Sally's comments on his care of Henrietta. "And if it's catching, she'd be sure to get it."

Dr. Dutch lifted his great head, with its shock of yellow hair. "I'm going to see vot is vot!" he declared.

He heaved himself to his knees, then slowly fell back in a faint.

John looked at Uncle Billy in a frightened way. "What can I do for you all, Uncle Billy? Are you able to feed yourselves?"

"Yes; so far I've been able to crawl out once a day and cook soup. It's all we're able to keep down. We're better than we were, and another week of quiet ought to see us through. You ought to have a good beating, John Sager— I don't see how you've made out. It beats anything I ever heard of!"

"Oh, we made out all right!" John tossed his head, determined not to show how his heart had sunk at the sight of the sick faces of these old friends. "Guess I'd better go out and make our camp. I'll get far enough away so the children can't bother you. And I'll bring you some soup as soon as Catherine can make it."

Again Aunt Sally sought to rise, but could only groan. "All those poor little children on our hands again!"

"They won't be on your hands long!" retorted John, turning on his heel.

He led his family to a camping-place at a good distance from the Shaws' tents.

"But this is awful lonesome," protested Francis.

"Well, I keep telling you they're awful sick. They both look like Mother and Father did. They just are scared to death at the thought of us seven young ones piling in on them, and they would be glad to half kill me." John could not resist a grin, as he added, "It's an ill wind that blows nobody any good!"

Francis returned the grin. "Meaning that their sickness is saving you a hard licking, I suppose."

John nodded and, the tent being up, took the baby from Catherine and turned to speak to the Indian, who was taking the packs from his ponies.

"Yellow Serpent, there's still enough daylight left for you to make some money. If you will cut a week's supply of fire-wood for Captain Shaw, he'll give you two dollars. Just haul over to his tent a lot of that dead and down pine on the cliff back of their camp."

The Indian nodded. His laziness disappeared at the mention of real money.

"And, Yellow Serpent," John went on, "those folks are too sick to travel. I must leave them here and take the baby on to the Whitmans'. Will you go on with me as guide?"

Yellow Serpent shook his head. "Won't go over Blue Mountains. Cayuse at Waii-lat-pu kill me."

"No, they won't. Dr. Whitman wouldn't let them!" exclaimed John.

"You talk like fool!" replied Yellow Serpent.

"I don't ask you to do it for nothing," urged John. "Back at Fort Hall, in the wagon I left there, is a box with white people's dishes. If you will guide us to the Whitmans', I'll give you a paper talk to Captain Grant and he'll give you the dishes." John was offering the things that he thought would tempt an Indian more than anything left in the wagon except the contents of the horsehair trunk. In this were packed all his mother's clothes and the little treasures that she had brought from home with her. John had decided that nothing on earth could make him give up that trunk.

But Yellow Serpent was not to be bribed. "No like Cayuse," he repeated. And when John urged him, he struck the boy on the cheek and walked away muttering.

John was startled. Yellow Serpent and his squaw had been pleasant enough on the trip from Fort Boise. To be sure, except in the crossing of the streams and packing and unpacking, they had allowed the children to do all the work, but their mere presence had been a great source of comfort. John had felt very sure, when he was making his

half-defiant statements to the Shaws, that Yellow
Serpent would go on with them. He walked back
to the fire Francis was kindling, filled with a new
anxiety.

Catherine, stirring the contents of the soup-kettle
with a long stick, greeted John with a rapturous
grin.

"Oh, isn't this a lovely place for a camp! Let's
stay—"

John interrupted her furiously. "Catherine, if you
say that again about a camp, I'll lick you! I'll bet
you've said it a hundred times—"

It was Catherine's turn to interrupt. "I never
have! We haven't been in that many pretty camps.
Most of them are horrible!"

"This is horrible, too," growled John, rocking the
baby gently in his arms and scowling at the beautiful stretch of grazing lands which formed the floor
of the Grande Ronde valley. Some careless camper
had allowed fire to burn off the dead grass of summer and now a fine crop of new grass covered the
ground.

"It's the prettiest spot we've been in," insisted
Catherine, "except those hot springs."

No immigrant, save John, ever had passed
through this circular valley without echoing Catherine's sentiments. About twenty miles wide, surrounded by mountains heavily covered with timber,

watered by fine streams that had produced a rich soil, it was a pioneer's ideal of a farm, except for one point. It was too difficult to reach either from east or west. But, come upon after the awful horrors of the Rocky Mountains, the Grande Ronde might well look like paradise to Catherine, or any other weary traveler over the Oregon Trail.

"What are you mad about now, old trapper?" asked Francis, observing John's scowl as he came up with an armload of wood.

John's scowl deepened. "I'm not mad. I'm worried. Listen to this," and he told them of Yellow Serpent's decision.

"Are there a lot of deep rivers to cross?" queried Francis.

"I don't think so," replied John. "But we've got to go over the Blue Mountains yonder"—pointing to the northwest—"and as far back as the Green River 'Rendezvous' they were talking about how hard that range was to cross. Once we're over, Mr. Mc-Kay said we're only twenty miles from the Whitmans' and easy going."

"Are you going off and leave Aunt Sally and Uncle Billy and Dr. Dutch to die here alone? And the wolves eat them up because no one buries them?" demanded Catherine. "After all they've done for us?"

John bit his lower lip, and his sigh was almost

like a sob. He was so tired of making these decisions
that dealt with life and death! Strange that before
his father and mother died he was always saying
that he was a man and thinking of himself as one.
And since their death, except when he was doing a
bit of boasting, he was always telling himself that it
was tough on a boy to have to think out grown-up
matters, and he now pictured himself as young—
very, very young.

He looked from Catherine to Francis and from
them to the bundle in his arms. "Look!" he said.

The three unkempt heads bent over Henrietta.
She managed a ghastly little smile that drew the
skin like white tissue-paper over the bones of her
cheeks. With a sob, Francis bent his frowzled red
head and kissed the tiny white claw that curled
against the baby's chin.

"Now we're in country where Betsy can get grass
regularly, maybe baby can keep more milk down,"
said John.

"Don't let Dr. Dutch tell you what to do!" exclaimed Francis. "He's killed two of our family.
That's enough."

"If we can get baby alive to Mrs. Whitman, we'll
save her," said John slowly, thinking aloud. "If we
stay here till the Shaws can travel, she'll surely die.
We can't do the Shaws any good. We'd worry 'em
about food and everything else. As long as there's no

big streams to cross, the Injuns couldn't do us any
real good, I suppose."

Francis suddenly sobbed aloud. "I'm scared of
being alone on the trail again!" Then, as poor John
threw back his head in the familiar impatient way,
Francis drew his naked little arm across his eyes,
swallowed hard and managed a grin. "All right,
old Pie Biter. I'm not standing in your way. On to
Oregon!"

"Good for you, old trapper!" John nodded. "Come
on, let's eat. I've got to fix things up with Uncle
Billy. Mind, you kids all keep away from their tent,
and if anybody does crawl out of there to talk to
you, don't breathe that the Injuns don't go on with
us. Or they'll never let us go."

As soon as supper was over, John crossed the
meadow to Uncle Billy's camp. He built a great fire
before the tent opening, then threw back the flap
and entered with his kettle of hot soup.

"My, that blaze does look cheerful," quavered
Aunt Sally, as John lifted her tin cup from its place
by her pillow and filled it with the broth.

"I told the Injun you'd give him two dollars if
he'd fix you up with enough wood for a week," said
John. "Did you hear him piling it? He says when the
moon comes up he and his squaw will cut it for
you."

"You show some real brains once in a while,

Johnny!" Uncle Billy took a long sip of the broth.
"By hominy, that's good! My soup's mostly water
because I couldn't gather wood to cook it long."

"Catherine's going to make you your ten-gallon
kettle full if you'll loan it to us," said John, giving
Dr. Dutch his portion. "Still believe in meat for folks
with dysentery, Doctor?"

"Ve are all done mit the disease," replied the
doctor. "Vat ve need now is to get back our strengt'.
Gott in Himmel! das ist gut! How haf you made it?"

"We got a quarter of beef from McKay and we
saved all our bones for it. Two days ago Yellow
Serpent shot a deer, and today Francis and I shot
three jack-rabbits. So there's beef-bone and venison
and rabbit in it."

"You mustn't use your meat for our soup," said
Aunt Sally. "We have a week's supply of beef and
flour. You must cut off a big piece of rump to go
with our soup. Catherine is getting to be a real cook.
Bless the child! Tomorrow, I want to see her. My,
but I do feel stronger already!"

"Have another cup." John ladled out the soup
with a generous hand. "We've got two rabbits left.
We'll put them into your pot and a good hunk of
venison along with the rump."

"I don't feel quite so much like licking you,
Johnny," said Uncle Billy, beginning his second

helping. "Not but what you deserve it, ten times over, eh, Doctor?"

Dr. Dutch was beginning his fourth cup. "Vell, I ain't responsible, right now, for vat I t'ink. This soup makes my heart soft."

"It's Catherine's soup," chuckled John. "But if it saves me hard feelings, she won't grudge my getting credit for it."

"Himmel, you are thin, Johnny!" exclaimed the doctor, raising himself on one elbow to stare at the boy in the firelight. "If you are so, vat must the little girls be!"

"They're all well!" declared John.

"We'll judge for ourselves in the morning," said Aunt Sally. "I want to see that baby. What's this idea about Mrs. Whitman?"

John sat down in the tent opening, where he could feed the fire and still talk with ease. Carefully avoiding any mention of the condition in which his little caravan had reached Fort Boise, he repeated what Mr. McKay had told him about Mrs. Whitman.

"And you plan to crash right on through to their mission," mused Uncle Billy. "Are these Indians reliable?"

"They have been, so far. Mr. McKay picked 'em and he's paying 'em. I'm to pay back when I get to earning money," replied John, hoping the questioning would go no further.

"I vill see the baby in the morning and judge."
Dr. Dutch took another sip of broth.

"I'll bet I fool you!" thought John. Aloud he said,
"How long before you'd be able to take care of her,
Aunt Sally?"

"I'm afraid it will be several days before my arms
get their strength, John," sighed Aunt Sally.

"And what could you do for her you didn't do
before, Doctor?"

"Let me tell you something, you folks!" Uncle
Billy broke in hoarsely. "A little peppermint and
castor-oil isn't going to do anything for that baby.
She needs to be under shelter in a house, with
quiet and with constant care, just like you give a
little sick lamb that's lost its mother. Johnny is a
young devil, but he's giving that baby its only
chance when he tries to get it in the hands of a
woman who's in a house with conveniences."

"William Shaw!" Aunt Sally got up on her elbow
and flung her braid of gray hair back over her
shoulder with a snap. "William Shaw, are you hinting that I couldn't take as good care of that baby as
that Whitman woman?"

"I'm not hinting at anything. I say, flat-footed,
that for a week you won't be fit to give her any
care at all and that she might better be in Mrs.

Whitman's hand at the end of that time than yours. Mrs. Whitman will have something to offer her and you won't."

"What do you mean by that?" demanded Aunt Sally.

"I mean just this, Sally. You act and talk as if you expected, when you reach the Willamette, to step into a fine house with all the comforts you left at home. Well, you ain't! This trip has taken just about everything we have, including our health and strength. Instead of reaching the Willamette with five hundred dollars in gold, a wagon-load of furniture, ten cows, a pair of oxen, and five horses, if we reach there at all, we'll be practically penniless, our furniture left beside the trail between here and Green River, the livestock eaten or stolen by the Indians. We'll have to live close till I can get a job and earn enough to build a house and get some farm tools together. You can't talk about taking a baby in, let alone six other growing children, not if there's a chance of someone else doing it."

Aunt Sally sank back with a groan.

"I know!" Uncle Billy put out a feeble, calloused hand and patted her shoulder. "It sounds hard. God knows, I wish we could take care of Henry Sager's children for him. I thought I could, but fate's been all against me. From what I hear, these Whitmans are good people, with a big, thriving farm. If they'll do for these children, they're in luck."

Uncle Billy sank wearily back on his pillow, and for many minutes there was no sound but the crackle of the fire. John felt dazed. Ever since his mother's death, however much he might defy the captain and his wife, they had been his people. However independent and self-important he might feel, still he had counted absolutely on their care and help. And now they had cast him off!

If they had measured out this decision as punishment for his defiance at Fort Hall and his running away, he would have felt hopeful. He'd have asked for a dozen lickings instead, and have cajoled them into helping him out with the children until he had made a home for them on that farm of his father's dream. But Uncle Billy's statement was not based on any desire to get even with him. It was based on the terrible necessities that faced the captain. And against the necessities that rose on the Oregon Trail, John knew there was no use in arguing.

He had never felt so lonely in his life; no, not even the night his father died, not even when he saw his mother laid in her brush-lined grave on Black Fork. For deep as had been his grief then, he had had no idea of what it meant for a boy to take on himself the responsibilities of a grown person. Now, he knew.

"Well," he said at last, "I must get back to the children. I'll bring the soup over tomorrow morning—will cut off a piece of rump now."

Dr. Dutch sat up. The tears were running down his cheeks and he tried to speak, but he couldn't. Aunt Sally sobbed into her blanket.

"The beef's hanging in the larch-tree, to the left," said Uncle Billy, brokenly.

"You've been awful good to us young ones, anyhow." John jerked the words out in an embarrassed way and left the tent.

## CHAPTER XIII

# The Blue Mountains

JOHN roused the children the next morning before daylight. He would not allow any of them to visit the Shaw tent, nor did he go in himself when he carried the soup to the camp. Long before sun-up he was leading the way over the Blue Mountain trail.

The children now had before them a journey

which well-equipped outfits ordinarily made in a few days. It differed from anything in the way of travel which they had met before because, for the first time, they were meeting with great forests, those marvelous woods of the Northwest like which there is nothing so wonderful in any other part of the United States.

Wonderful, yes, those fine trees, with trunks as thick as John was tall, those larches and birch of a size suited to a giant's park; wonderful, but, oh, how difficult for young feet to travel under. After the first day there was snow; there was chaos of wooded canyons and meadow-like valleys; there were bitter winds and lurking forms of wolves and wildcats.

They started with a week's supply of meat, which was fortunate, for there was very little ammunition. And they started with John depressed by Captain Shaw's decision, and with the nestlings, as Dr. Dutch once called the younger children, bewildered and frightened because they were leaving behind Uncle Billy and Aunt Sally, whom they had thought of as a father and mother.

But, in spite of all their handicaps, they did fairly well for the first three days. During the fourth night, something wakened John. He was sleeping with the baby snuggled against his chest. For a moment, as his eyes flew open, he dared not put his cheek to

her lips, as he did so frequently now, for fear she
might have died. Perhaps she had struggled with
death, he told himself, and so had roused him. Then,
as he wakened more thoroughly, he lifted the blanket from the little face. A faint warmth on his cold
cheek. She was still living, thank God!

But still he could not sleep. Strange, for he was
very tired and weak from overwork. Before the tent
there was still a faint glow of live coals, for they
had put two huge logs on before going to bed. John
crept from beneath the blankets and looked at his
father's watch. It was three o'clock. He threw another log on the fire and by its blaze peered into the
tent to see if all were well with the children.

The "twins," Elizabeth and Louisa, were snuggled
on either side of Francis. John pulled the blankets
well up about them, then peered beneath the covers
where Catherine and Matilda—

Matilda was not there!

John rummaged beneath all the blankets. Matilda
was gone! He shook Francis and Catherine into
wakefulness. Rubbing their eyes and shivering, they
staggered out to the fire.

"Injuns?" mumbled Francis.

"Where's Matilda?" cried Catherine.

"Did you just miss her?" demanded John. Then,
not waiting for an answer to his question, he seized
a blazing branch of balsam. "Help me search! Keep

calling! Don't get out of sight of the fire. Each of you take a torch!"

The camp had been made in a forest of pine, through the high branches of which little snow had sifted. The three children ran to and fro, calling continuously.

"Matilda! Matilda! Matilda!"

After a half-hour of this, they came back to the fire, wearied out and all but voiceless. Catherine was sobbing, and even John's face worked as he said:

"We—we'll heat some soup. She might wander in."

"She—she—she's frozen to death by now!" sobbed Catherine.

"Aw, shut up, old Calamity Jane," snarled Francis, "if you can't think of something else to say!" He was warming first one half-naked foot, then the other, at the fire, pulling a bit of wolfskin over his shoulders.

"I suppose she walked in her sleep," said John huskily. "It's a wonder none of us have done it before. I never thought of it, or I'd 'a' fastened up the flap every night. Come, old lady, quit crying into the soup-pot. We'll find her. She's too little to have got very far. If the wolves—" He stopped, gulped, and took up his gun. "You two rest till I get back. I'm going down to the meadow where we staked Thunder and old Betsy and Silas. I'm afraid the wolves might have bothered them. I heard wolves before I went to sleep."

He remembered, indeed, that some time during the night he had heard wolves snarling over a kill. Sick with fear, he wondered if it was this that had really wakened him. With a blazing pine-knot in one hand and his gun in the other, he made his way through the heavy brush and fallen timber toward the little meadow where the stock was pastured. But long before he reached the pasture he came upon the kill. Thunder, the pony, had pulled up his stake, had started for the tent, had fallen or had been pulled down, and his poor old body had made a meal for a wolf-pack.

Evidently the wolves had been frightened away before their ghastly meal was finished by the lights and shouts of the search for Matilda. John paused only for a hurried glance, then, full of terrible foreboding, he rushed on toward the meadow.

Silas was standing, knee-deep in brown grass, chewing as contentedly as if his great ribs were not all but protruding from his hide, his great spine sagging with weakness. Just beyond him was old Betsy. She, too, was contentedly chewing the cud, but she was lying down to do it, saving the remnant of her strength, like the sensible bossy she was. John flashed his torch, first at Silas, then at Betsy. There was a red lump—a mass of yellow hair—

"Matilda!" John gave a great shout.

Sound asleep in a comfortable ball against Betsy's warm but bony side, lay the little girl. John dropped his gun and pounced upon her. She opened her eyes long enough to smile.

"Johnny! I wented back to Aunt Sally!" Then she buried her nose in John's neck.

He kissed her frowzy hair; then, with a queer little quiver of his chin, he stooped and kissed old Betsy on her forehead. She blinked her great eyes at him, but never stopped chewing. Nothing that the Sager children could do could astonish Betsy.

It was a long carry back to the camp, but, somehow, John made it—gun, torch and little girl. Matilda was pathetically light for a three-year-old. He shouted as soon as he caught sight of the fire, and Francis and Catherine came running.

"You feed her plenty of hot soup," ordered John, as Catherine devoured the child with kisses. "She's shaking with cold. And then you tie her leg to yours, when you get back into bed. Francis and I've got to go for Betsy and Silas before the wolves get them, too."

It was five o'clock before the boys had tethered the cattle within the circle of the firelight, but both boys were so tired that John dared not start the day's work until they had rested. They heaped more logs on the fire and went to bed.

Matilda naturally had a heavy cold as a result of her exposure. She was croupy and feverish when John examined her after their late breakfast.

"Let's rest for the day and see if we can't break it up," suggested Francis.

John looked from Matilda to Henrietta. Was ever a boy confronted with such a choice? "Very well," he said at last, "but I don't like it."

"I do!" sighed Catherine. "I got chilblains worse than any of you."

Elizabeth, crouching beside the fire, sucking a rabbit-bone and crying as the warmth of the fire tormented her frost-bitten hands, burst into sudden speech. She was ordinarily a very silent child.

"I'm not going a step on! I'm going to wait here for Aunt Sally!"

"Me, too!" piped Louisa, whose swollen little feet Catherine was rubbing with tallow.

John grunted, but said nothing. It had not occurred to him that the children ever could seriously oppose his will. He dosed Matilda with hot broth and kept her smothered in blankets until she sweated and her hot cheeks were cool. Then he spanked her because she insisted on getting up to play. He had just finished this fatherly chore when an Indian rode into camp.

He jumped off his pony, wrapped a red blanket around him, and approached the group huddled near the fire. He was a young brave with a painted face that started the "twins" to crying. John hushed them with a scowl.

"Hello, stranger!" he said.

"How!" replied the Indian. "You the big chief boss the little squaws?"

"Yes, if you like it that way. I don't!" replied John crossly. He was too tired to be alarmed.

"You good trail chief," the Indian went on with a grin. "You lose white trail, two sleeps back. You on Injun trail now. Injun trail better trail."

John felt more cheerful. He had not known of this change of trail, but he was not going to admit it. He was feeling badly in need of praise, was poor John.

"Want to eat?" he asked.

"Heap hungry," nodded the brave. "Here's your paper talk. You make another paper talk. Then White Belly turn back."

He handed the astonished John a letter.

Dear John:
You are a white man and a scout. Señorita arrived fine. We leave now for Santa Fé to be married. We'll see you in the summer when I come through with Lieutenant Frémont. You turned the trick.
                    Yours truly,
                    CHRISTOPHER CARSON.

John spelled out the note, then stared at the Indian. "Where did you get this?"

White Belly, his mouth full of rabbit, shook his head. "No can tell anybody anything. You make paper talk, tell him how you come. Sabe?"

"I can get bark for you to write on, John!" cried Francis, anxious to show off a little of his hard-earned Indian lore. As he spoke, he shuffled away among the trees on his frost-bitten feet. He returned shortly with a six-inch square of unmarred birch-bark.

John wrote with his knife-point:

Dear Mr. Carson:
I am glad you are glad. I and my family are doing pretty good.
Yours truly,
JOHN SAGER.

He gave this to White Belly, then pointed at the Indian's horse.

"You have a good pony. You help me get the papooses to Whitman mission. See my cattle!" He pointed to Betsy and Silas, munching dried grass the children had gathered. They were living skeletons.

White Belly shook his head. "Me, Ute Injun. If go over to Cayuse camp, lose scalp."

John sighed, and shook his head at Catherine, who began to sob. "You have a swift pony. You ride

in the night to Dr. Whitman, ask him to come quick
and meet me on the trail with my sick papooses. If
you'll do this, I'll send paper talk by you to Captain
Grant and tell him to give you the dishes in our
covered wagon."

White Belly stared. "You got 'em covered wagon
at Fort Hall?"

"Yes," replied John.

"How you mean dishes?"

Francis made eager gestures, giving a picture of
the uses of chinaware.

White Belly nodded. "How many dishes?"

"You can have two cups, two plates, and the
saucers," replied John, who would have given him
all of the dishes in the sudden feeling of relief that
came to him. "Francis, get me some more birchbark,
will you?"

John wrote the letter to Captain Grant, the children watching him no more breathlessly than did
the Indian. When it was done, the Ute rolled it in a
corner of his blanket and tied it there with a leather
thong from his deerskin tunic.

"Good you stop here," he said. "Little way back
White Belly say to self, this Cayuse country. If no
see little white chief today, White Belly turn back."

"There!" cried Catherine. "Supposing I hadn't
made you stay!"

"Guess we'll have to give you credit," grunted

John, "though you hadn't any idea you were doing anything but getting a rest."

"Just like you hadn't any idea you were off the Oregon Trail!" retorted Catherine.

"You talk too much!" exclaimed John, turning to the Ute, who was listening with a broad grin. "Are you afraid to start now, White Belly?" he asked.

The Indian looked through the tall trunks of the pines, where dusk was falling.

"No! Start now!" he replied.

He leaped to his pony's back and was gone like a blowing leaf.

The children took a long night's sleep. The next morning dawned clear and crisp and John had little difficulty in getting an early start with his charges. Everyone was in fine spirits. Within two days, at the latest, they were certain Dr. Whitman would find them. In fact, John himself was so sure of it that had not this been a dry camp, he would have waited for the doctor there. His plan was to move on till they found a good camping-place and remain there.

So all day they moved up and down the shoulders of the mountain, slowly, for the cattle were staggering with weakness. Near sunset they emerged from the forest into a little meadow through which rushed a mountain brook. The wind had blown the snow away in many spots, leaving good pasturage.

"Here's White Belly's tracks again," said Francis,

for they had followed the Ute's pony at intervals all day. "Shall we camp by the brook or under the trees, John?"

"Water's easier to carry than wood, stupid," replied John, lifting Matilda and Louisa from their baskets while Francis began to unpack the tent from old Betsy's back. "Here, hand me the ax. You get a pail of water," as the animals, freed of their burden, staggered eagerly to graze.

"I'd rather chop and get warm," pleaded Francis.

"All right." John picked up the bucket without protest. Surely this was a different boy from the sulky cub on the Platte who had fought over chores and been disobliging to his mother. Responsibility is a great teacher.

He dragged his swollen feet along the track made by the Ute's horse toward a clump of willows by the brook. Just at the edge of the brook lay a brown heap. With a strange sinking of his heart, John drew near—

Naked and scalped, White Belly lay dead in the snow.

How long he stood shivering, John did not know. The one clear thought in his mind was that the children must not discover this. Somehow, he must hide the Ute's body. He was shaking so that he could hardly hold the pail in his hands, but he fought for self-control and at last he scooped up a pailful of snow and flung it over the Indian. Then he worked frantically till the body was well covered. Before he had finished, he heard Catherine calling him. She worried when any one of the children was out of sight.

John shouted in reply and a few minutes later filled the bucket with water and panted back to the camp. A good fire was going and Francis was struggling with the tent.

"Thought you'd got hurt," said Francis.

"Was looking around," mumbled John. "Lemme warm my hands and I'll help you."

"Looks like we could only make this meat last one more day," announced Catherine; "but that don't matter. Tomorrow night, by this time, Dr. Whitman'll be here."

"I hope he won't stop to hunt on the way!" exclaimed Francis. "I'll try to pop some bunnies tomorrow. What's the matter with you, John? You look sick!"

"I do feel kind of squeamish in my stomach," replied John.

"Gosh!" Francis' great eyes in his little thin face grew even larger. "Don't *you* get sick on us, Johnny! What on earth would we do!"

John grinned feebly. "It ain't that kind of sickness. I'll be well as soon as I get warm."

"Anyway, if you do get sick," said Catherine, "Dr.

Whitman'll take care of you. This is a lovely camp to be sick in."

Francis chuckled. John, warming his shaking hands, spoke with unusual gentleness. "Don't gab so much, Catherine. Heat baby's milk, right away. Let me have the ax, Francis. I'm going to keep a fire going, tonight, that'll melt the snow off this whole mountain."

Undoubtedly, it was this easy supply of fuel, during the latter part of their journey, that made it possible for the younger children, at least, to come through alive. The dead timber, so easy to roll into the flames, seemed to have been placed at hand by the kindness of Providence itself.

After supper John felt better, though he could not keep his mind off that ghastly bloody heap by the willows. Finally, he brought out the Bible.

"This isn't Sunday," protested Francis.

"I've lost track of what day it is," retorted John, "but I'm going to read the Prayer of Habakkuk, just the same."

The younger children were asleep in the tent. Francis and Catherine, blinking with weariness, sat with owlish blue eyes on him while he read again the immortal words:

*"O Lord, I have heard thy speech and was afraid: O Lord, revive thy work in the midst of the years,*

*in the midst of the years made known: in wrath
remember mercy."*

The strange and magnificent words comforted
him, and he slept the dreamless sleep of exhaustion
that night.

After breakfast the next morning, he told the children that he was determined, because of the scar-
city of food, to move on. Francis and Catherine at
first flat-footedly refused to do so. John tried to
tease them into going, but when this had no effect,
he pretended to fly into a terrible rage and threat-
ened to beat them. It was not long before they were
sulkily following him along the trail that led once
more into the forest.

In camp that night, by a spring that trickled
among icicles over a black rock, with a great grove
of balsam-pine sighing about them, the younger
children, even little Matilda, managed to keep
awake two hours later than usual, listening for Dr.
Whitman. John made no protest, but he had hard
work to keep the tears back as he sat with the baby
in his lap, forcing, now and again, a few drops of
warm milk between her little blue lips. It seemed to
him that at times she did not breathe. But he could
not be sure, for he was very, very tired. He thought
that three more days surely must bring them to the
mission, but he could not be sure of this either, for

the cattle were in such bad shape that he could no longer make calculations based on their speed.

Somehow, the next day, he started the little cavalcade on its way again.

Toward mid-afternoon, as they were climbing a steep ridge, poor old Silas sighed, settled gently on his knees and died.

Then came a real revolt on the part of the children. They huddled around Silas, weeping bitterly, crouched like stricken lambs, and refused to move.

John stood beside old Betsy, staring at the sad little group, his eyes dim with tears, but with jaws set in knots. His determination to keep going, in the face not only of all the sufferings of the trail, but with the children's increasing opposition, is almost unbelievable. Most children of thirteen keep on doing their duty, only as their parents drag and drive them on. John himself, before Naomi and Henry Sager died, was a good example of that kind of child.

But John had a reason for keeping on that the other children were too young to understand. John was carrying on his father's dream.

"Don't you want that farm on the Willamette?" he demanded fiercely.

A wordless wail from Francis answered him.

"Very well!" shouted John hoarsely. "I've kept it from you all this time, but now I'll tell you. You've made me do it, you pack of cowards! The day after

White Belly left us I found his body *dead* by the brook. He had an arrow in his heart and I covered him with snow. He never reached the mission, and the only way we'll see the Whitmans is to never stop going as long as I tell you to keep going."

A dead silence greeted this. John repeated the statement so distinctly that even little Matilda, still seated in her basket against old Silas's ribs, understood him. After a while, Francis wiped his nose on the piece of blanket that did service for his coat, and said:

"What things do we leave behind us, Johnny?"

A day later, a little group of children emerged from the trees that covered the last western crest of the Blue Mountains and stood gazing into a vast valley. The snow was blood-stained beneath their feet. Behind them, chaos of range and canyon over which they had crept like tiny snails. Before them, a wide plain of rolling brown hills, cut by little streams like silver hairs, and by a wide black-and-silver ribbon that John was sure was the Columbia. He allowed the nestlings a moment in which to shiver, to look, to whimper; then, with fumbling feet, he moved down the mountainside. His bare feet were tied up with pieces of buffalo-hide. His long yellow hair was bound back from his eyes by a twist of leather round his forehead. On his back

was Matilda; in his arms, Henrietta, motionless as death, in a wolfskin.

Staggering back of John was old Betsy, her hoofs split to the quick, moaning as she moved. On her back huddled Catherine with five-year-old Louisa. Francis, his gray eyes dull, buckskin pants reduced to a mere clout, red flannel shirt only a fluttering decoration across his chest, brought up the rear, dragging Elizabeth.

Stumbling, rising, panting, they made their way down into the plains. They camped that night only a few miles from the Whitman mission.

The trail in the valley was broad and dusty. It was warm, too, like spring. The children needed little urging on that last day, and John was able to give all his attention to the baby. The last mile he could not be sure that she was alive. For two days she had not uttered a sound.

"I see it!" exclaimed Catherine, late in the after-noon.

John lifted his cheek from Henrietta's lips. A long, low house behind a fence seemed to lie across the trail, at the foot of the little hill they had just topped. Someone seemed to sight the children, too, for a woman came out of the door and stood with a hand shading her eyes.

Slowly, so slowly through the dust, until suddenly, as if she had only now recognized their weakness, the woman opened the gate and ran to meet them.

"Children! Children!" she cried. "Who are you?"

She was very tall. She had braids of yellow hair wrapped around her head. Catherine, writing so many years later, says she seemed to the children even more beautiful than their mother.

"We're the Sager family," said John. "Mother and Father died. Here's our baby!"

With a little cry, Narcissa Whitman held out her arms. Then, as she turned back the wolfskin and looked at what lay beneath, she groaned. A big bearded man came hurrying up and looked with her, while the other children waited in breathless silence.

"She's not dead yet," said Dr. Whitman, at last. "Rush her into a warm bath, Narcissa, while I attend to the rest of this little wolf-pack." He turned with a smile and plucked Matilda from John's back. "Come with me to the cabin, children, while I see what's to be done first to turn you into human beings."

But John did not heed the doctor. He followed Mrs. Whitman into the living-room of the mission and crouched before the fire, watching her every move while young Henrietta was laid for a moment in warm water, then rubbed in hot oil, wrapped in soft wool and placed on Mrs. Whitman's lap. And all this while, the baby showed no sign of life save an uncertain warmth that appeared in her spider-like hands.

After watching her pulse for a moment, Mrs. Whitman began to drop hot, diluted milk between the blue lips and gently to chafe the little throat. After what seemed a long, long time, the throat contracted and a whimper, something less than a mouse's squeak, came forth. At this sound John threw himself forward, wrapped his arms about Mrs. Whitman's knees, and began to cry.

She put her hand on his shaggy head. "What is your name, my dear?" she said.

"John. Will she live?"

"We'll fight for her and pray for her. Will you go out and send the doctor to me, and get yourself fed and cleaned?"

John gave a great sigh. "I knew if I could just get her to you—" he murmured and limped out the door.

He found the children in a cabin near the main house. Dr. Whitman was feeding the three littlest girls with cornmeal gruel and milk, while Catherine and Francis were dressing themselves under the direction of a thin, middle-aged woman the doctor called Mrs. Munger.

"Gosh, John!" cried Francis. "See these clothes

Mrs. Munger got out of the missionary barrel for me! Doctor says I can keep them!"

"How is baby?" asked Catherine, smoothing the skirt of a red calico dress.

"Better," replied John.

"Drink a bowl of that hot broth, John," ordered Dr. Whitman; "then go into the ell, where you'll find a tub of water. When you're clean you can fill up on gruel."

"Thank you, sir. Mrs. Whitman wants you, please."

The doctor rose. "Mrs. Munger, put these three little girls to bed in the bunks, here, as soon as they're fed. John, you bring your brother and sister up to the mission house as soon as you're washed and fed."

"Yes, sir," replied John.

But, after all, John returned to the mission house alone, for Catherine and Francis were asleep by the time John had finished his supper, and Mrs. Munger would not permit him to wake them. He found the doctor and his wife sitting before the fire in their bedroom, the baby still in Mrs. Whitman's lap. They both smiled as John came in. Mrs. Munger had clipped his hair, and he wore a shabby but neat blue suit, sent by the missionary society of some Eastern church to this outpost in the West. He explained the absence of the younger children.

"Well! Well! You look so's your folks would recognize you again, I guess!" exclaimed Dr. Whitman. "Think I got most of your story from Francis and Catherine. A wonderful job you've done, my boy. We're a thousand miles from South Pass, about where you first took over your job, as near as I can calculate. Surely, the Lord has led you on!"

Mrs. Whitman caught John by the hand and pulled him toward her. "You are thinner than any living child has a right to be, John. You are a brave, brave boy. I wish your mother and father had been here to welcome you." She pulled him down to her and kissed his forehead. Then she said to her husband, "Marcus, he's feverish!"

"Excited, I guess," replied the doctor. "Too excited to sleep for a while, aren't you, John?"

"Yes, sir. I gotta know if you will take care of the baby till I can fix a place for us in the Willamette Valley. Then will you promise to give her back to me, and how much will you charge?"

The doctor looked from John's haggard features to his wife's Madonna face, and his great voice was very gentle as he said, "Get into that big chair, John," pointing to one covered with buffalo-hide at the right side of the fire. "We'll talk it all over. Francis told me about Captain Shaw. Did you plan to go to them? They'll be coming through in a day or so, I suppose."

John shook his head. "They can't take us—seven of us—just the two youngest, and I promised my mother I'd keep the children together. And, anyhow, I've got to do my father's job."

"What job is that?" asked Dr. Whitman.

John found it not too difficult to talk to these kindly people, and little by little he told them many of the things that had been in his mind since that day on the Platte when he had run away. He did not tell his thoughts very clearly, but the missionaries understood better than you or I would have, because they lived in a pioneer's world. You and I will never hear that magic call of the West, "Catch up! Catch up! Catch up!" We never shall see the Rockies framed in the opening of our prairie schooner and tingle with the knowledge that if we and our fellow immigrants can reach the valleys in the blue beyond the mountains and there plow enough acreage, that acreage will belong forever to America.

But the Whitmans had heard and seen and felt all this, and so they understood John's stuttering, blurred sentences. When he at last had finished telling them what was in his heart, the doctor put a great hand on the boy's shoulder.

"If the baby lives," he said huskily, "we'll see what we can do to help you. Now go to bed, John."

"I can't go away from the baby!" protested John.

"Let me roll in a blanket here on the floor, please do!"

So John slept on the floor beside Mrs. Whitman, while the doctor dozed in the big chair. But Mrs. Whitman sat wide awake, watching and tending the little being in her lap.

What thoughts passed through her mind that night we do not know, although her diary tells what she did for the baby. We may be fairly sure that she thought much of her own little drowned baby, her only child, and we know that great love and pity came out of that night of watching and thinking, for at dawn she roused the doctor and asked him if he would be willing to keep the children at the mission.

"I must have the baby," she said with a little smile, "and it's evident that John will not permit the baby to be separated from the others."

"Seven of them, Narcissa!" gasped the doctor. "Do you realize what you're saying? Seven!"

"We're feeding sixteen *Indian* orphans and schooling them," replied Mrs. Whitman. "Aren't these little souls quite as important?"

"And, except the two oldest, quite as wild," said Dr. Whitman grimly. "Well, as you say, seven added to sixteen won't make much difference. The brunt of it falls on you. The decision should rest with you."

"I've thought and prayed about it all night," said

Mrs. Whitman. "I'm convinced that this is the Lord's wish."

"Then let's rouse the boy and tell him his journey's at an end." The doctor leaned over and shook John.

He sat up blinking. "Baby worse?"

"No; decidedly better. She kept down the last teaspoonful of milk. But it will take months of the greatest care to bring back her strength, and by that time I'll love her so, I shan't want to give her up." Mrs. Whitman spoke seriously.

John scowled. How selfish women were about a baby! he thought. He'd supposed Mrs. Whitman understood how it was with him. She was smiling at him now, as she went on:

"And so, as I must take care of the baby, and must keep her, and as you must not let the children be separated, there seems no way out but for you all to stay and let us be father and mother to you all."

John drew a long breath. He looked at the two kind faces, at the comfortable room, and out the window at the wide fields dotted with corn-shocks.

"It's—it's like refusing to come into heaven," he said at last, his lips quivering. "But you know I *can't* stop. I've got to get on to the Willamette!"

"John," said the doctor, "hasn't anyone told you that the Government won't allow you to take up a homestead at your age?"

"No!" gasped the boy.

"Here's another thing. There are hundreds and hundreds of immigrants in the Willamette Valley looking for work which will support themselves and their families until they can make their farms support them. There's not nearly enough work for those grown men. What chance would a boy your age have?"

John sat huddled in his blanket, his eyes tragic. "What would my father say if I gave up his plan! I just can't do it!"

"There's plenty of work here for an active boy," the doctor went on. "The Indians are almost worthless. You and Francis can more than earn your board and schooling. I'll keep strict account, and when you are eighteen, you can go to the Willamette with horses and cattle and farm implements. Doesn't that sound like sense to you?"

John looked at the doctor doubtfully.

"And I have an idea," Mrs. Whitman took up the argument, "that when Kit Carson and Lieutenant Frémont come through here next year, they will be glad to see to it that an arrangement is made with the Government to hold land for you."

John's heart gave a great leap of hope and conviction. "I'm sure they would!" he cried. " 'Specially Kit Carson! I got him a wife, I guess!" with a sudden grin.

"Then you will stay?" asked Mrs. Whitman.

Before John could reply, Catherine, splendid in red calico, limped into the room. "We've had breakfast," she said. "How's baby? O John! This is just the loveliest place for a—a—"

"All right!" exclaimed John. "All right! We're going to stay right here. For once, you're going to have your wish!"

Catherine clasped her thin little hands, staring from one person to the other, utterly bewildered.

"Come here, dear, and I'll explain, while John goes for his breakfast," said Mrs. Whitman.

And safe in the circle of that tender arm, Catherine learned that the wonderful, the terrible journey on which John had led them had ended in the safe heaven of this home.